EASTERN MEN

By

Jim Christina

ISBN-13:
978-1453820346

ISBN-10:
1453820345

Black Dog Books
Simi Valley, CA

Other works by Jim Christina

The Hunter

Requiem For an Appaloosa

The Rights of Men

Stryker

An Evening with Tom Horn

FOREWARD

As the stories come, a thought occurs to me, and that thought is, do people really like these stories because they are good solid tales, or because they are my friends and family. Not able to answer that particular question on my own, I will leave it alone and hope it is because of the fore and not the latter.

This story is the story of Phineas Bellflower a writer coming to Arizona to see for himself the troubles the territory has been experiencing and because he is being pursued by two thugs from Brooklyn, New York, Spats Melloy and Mr. O'Brien. Both Spats and Mr. O'Brien work for the boss of the Fifth Ward, one Michael McManus a man of nefarious means and talents and consequently; rules the Fifth Ward with strong-arm tactics, murder and corruption. Bellflower wrote an expose' of McManus and because of the repercussions, fled New York a step in front of the two thugs.

Arriving in Tucson aboard a stagecoach, Bellflower meets and hires our old friends, Whitey Wellford and Lenny Bristol and together they set out on an easy trip to Tombstone. But as with everything else they try, Whitey and Lenny can't seem to get it right and Phineas Bellflower finds himself robbed, tied and left to die in the Sonora Desert. The story then becomes one of survival and learning to not fight the desert as Spats and Mr. O'Brien soon learn

This story is a lot lighter than any of the others as the Hunter and Stryker try to teach Bellflower the way of the desert and how to survive. I had a ball writing this story and often found myself laughing out loud at a conversation or comment made by any one of a number of characters. But the trek is still arduous and fraught with peril as it is taking place during one of the big renegade Apache outbreaks from the San Carlos reservation.

So, settle back with some coffee, a rainy night, light a fire and crack open "Eastern Men" I am sure you will enjoy it as well as the others and as much as I did while writing it.

JC

Simi Valley, California
October, 2010

AKNOWLEDGMENTS

It's fair to say that the amount of people getting involved in writing this book kept growing, but more, the amount of folks that have continually asked when this one was going to be done. Fans! I actually have fans. Never before have I felt the thrill that comes over one when a fan is asking when the next book is going to be done. It lends credence to the tales and to the characters in them and to the craft in writing them. Oh, I am no fool, I know they are not perfect and that's okay. They are what they are…easy fun reads designed to export knowledge of an age and of men hardened by the time, the life and the territory.

So, it is with that in mind, I now want to thank all of you, my fans, for the support, critiques, ideas and just plain good-natured ribbing. And, with the publishing of "Eastern Men" the Hunter and Stryker and the rest of the boys from both ranches and the desperados they are destined to meet will be on hiatus. Oh, I will be working on a new book, an excerpt will be in the rear just like always, but don't look for the newest book to be available until late spring of 2011.

Again, thank all of you for responding as you have, it is what keeps the Hunter Tales fresh and still coming, and a special thanks to Peter Conway for providing a model for

Phineas Bellflower on the cover. I have to say, he is one patient man.

jc

Eastern Men

PROLOGUE

Phineas Bellflower stepped from the stagecoach immediately turning to catch his bag that had already been thrown from the top of the coach hitting him square on the top of his bowler. It had become an ongoing joke between him and the driver since getting on the stage in Denver and Phineas had been hit squarely on his head exactly fourteen times. It had ceased to be funny thirteen times ago.

Phineas Bellflower was a writer and he was in Tucson to write about the Territory of Arizona. They had all heard so much since the street fight in Tombstone, he felt the need to come out and see for himself. He could have taken the train, which would have been easier on him and taken far less time, but he felt the experience of riding the vaunted stagecoach would give him a taste of the West that he needed to write his book and it would afford him the opportunity to put distance between him and two unsavory characters lurking in his past.

One thing he was discovering that was different from Chicago was the dust and dirt. Everything was coated with a fine layer of dust and it got into your eyes, nose and even your mouth. No one seemed to bother with it though as if they were either resigned or so used to it, it had ceased to be a bother to them at all.

Gathering up his bag, he crossed the street heading toward the Arizona Metropolitan Saloon. When he got to the door, he dusted himself off and walked through the door. At the bar a man stood wiping glasses, obviously a barman and there was a table of sandwiches and, what appeared to be, potato salad at the far end of the bar.

Phineas walked to the bar clearing his throat so the bartender would recognize he was there. The bartender looked up at him and continued his wiping.

"Excuse me sir. May I order a libation?" Phineas unbuttoned his coat and fished some money from his vest pocket.

"A libation? I ain't heard that since the Baron lit out from the territory," the barman walked to Phineas. "What kin I getcha?"

"A scotch, neat." Phineas answered.

"Bourbon, rye or Irish are yer choices," the bartender said.

"Then rye it is," said Phineas. He held out his hand. "Phineas Bellflower sir. Late of Chicago, now, apparently of Tucson...for the time being anyway."

Eastern Men

"Pearly," said the barman. "Just plain Pearly…late of Tucson, always to Tucson, probly die here in the Metro, in fuckin Tucson." They shook hands. "Nice ta meet ya. So, Phineas, whatcha doin in Tucson…most folks scramble ta get outta Tucson…and here you are actually coming here on purpose."

"Well, Pearly, I am a writer. We have heard so much about Arizona that I had to come see for myself, see if I can't write a book about the territory. Maybe travel to Tombstone, get a feel for the troubles there," he took a drink of his rye and put the glass back on the bar. "Where's a good hotel?"

"Probly best bet is the Grand down Stone Avenue. Not far from here, you just go out the door and turn right. When you get to Mesa St. turn left then turn left on Stone before you get to the livery…you get there ya gone too far." Pearly picked up his bar rag. "Y'all done?"

"I am, and I thank you sir." Phineas downed his rye. "Oh, by the way, anyone you would recommend as a guide?"

"Well, yea, but they ain't here jest now…fella by the name a Hunter and his partner Jeff Stryker," he said.

"Thank you again." Phineas turned and walked back outside turning to his right and walking down the sidewalk.

Eastern Men

Two men that had been leaning against the wall pushed off and followed him, stopping him when he turned left onto Mesa St.

"'Scuse me sir...you was lookin fer a guide? Me and my pard, Lenny, here would be happy to guide ya wherever ya want." Whitey Wellford hooked his thumbs into the top of his trousers.

"Sure enough would," chimed in Lenny Bristol. "We're top-notch guides I tell ya. Whitey's right, we'll take ya anyplace...anyplace at all."

Phineas eyed them for a brief period before answering. "Well, I am looking for a guide and two would be better than one, and since this Hunter fellow isn't available...all right gentlemen it's a deal."

"Where ya stayin?" Whitey picked up Phineas' bag. "Be happy ta help ya sir...and doncha worry, ya jest pay us what ya think we're worth. That's all...Yessir, that's all," he elbowed Lenny.

"Yessir, anything at all," parroted Lenny.

"Well then to the Grand, gentlemen," said Phineas and he was thrilled his Arizona adventure had started. He had yet to know, however, how much an adventure it was going to become.

Eastern Men

Eastern Men

ONE

Jeff Stryker sat back in his saddle. The ridge he sat on was one of many in the area where they were looking for Syrus Common. The Hunter and Stryker had lost his track almost a week ago in the country around them. To their south lay Skeleton Canyon, notorious for hiding desperados and whereas Syrus Common was no desperado, he was someone they were looking for as a favor to Dick Gird and Ed Schieffelin. The expanse to Stryker's front was filled with cactus, rocks, ridges and deep ravines, a perfect place to hide if you didn't want to get caught. They didn't know why Gird and Schieffelin wanted Common, and really didn't care. Their job was not to question, it was to find the prey.

Satisfied he was going to see nothing, Stryker turned his horse, Waco, and rode back down the ridge where the Hunter waited for him.

"Nuthin huh?" the Hunter was just hanging his canteen back on his saddle.

"Nuthin I could see anyhow," answered Stryker. "Could be he lit out for New Mexico, or meybe even Mexico." He stepped from his horse and pulled a stone from Waco's right front foot. Leaning against his saddle, he looked at the Hunter and sighed. "We been out here three weeks now with nary a trace a this fella…what's Mr. Gird want him fer anyhow?"

"Don't know, Jeff…that ain't our business. We can't find him, we can't find him, but we owe it to Dick Gird to look." The Hunter looked over to the left at a ridge they had been up and down a thousand times already. "Let's do one more wider sweep around this area and see if we can find this lad's tracks…they gotta be here somewhere," he thought for a moment. "Take the south pass and I'll take the north…swing a lot wider, let's find this feller."

Stryker struck off to the south around the ridge and swung wide going almost two miles out, hoping to cut the trail of Sy Common. He rode for nearly two hours when his eye caught an indent by a stone. He dismounted and looked and at an angle saw a lot more leading northeast. He pulled his Winchester from his rifle boot and fired three shots into the air then walked off to wait for the Hunter in some shade.

Thirty minutes later, he saw the Hunter riding around a mesa about three miles distant. He took a drink from his canteen and got more comfortable in the shade, waiting another ten minutes before he mounted and rode out to meet the Hunter.

When he got within earshot, he hallooed the Hunter. "Found em!"

Eastern Men

The Hunter visibly let out a sigh of relief. They would catch Sy Common after all. He rode up to Stryker. "Where did ya find em? Hell, Jeff, we looked everywhere."

"Yessir, but you was right, a little farther out is all we needed. Caught em a ways back…they head northeast." Stryker Looked at the Hunter. "You thinkin a goin now?"

"Yea, I'm thinkin just that. Let's go get packed up and catch that fellas track. The Hunter turned Bandit and headed back to their camp that was almost ten miles distant. Stryker turned Waco and trotted after the Hunter until he caught up to him. They rode the rest of the ride in relative easy silence.

The Hunter called a halt. Breaking away from Stryker, he climbed a hill, dismounted and took out his long glass. Peering into the distance, he saw a lone rider approaching the face of a small mesa. He watched him for some time until Stryker finally joined him on the hill.

"Think that's him?" Stryker asked.

"Dunno, maybe. He's too far to tell, but we keep on, we'll be close enough by nightfall. " The Hunter put his long glass away in his saddlebags. "Seems a shame someone feels they gotta run when it ain't real hard to toe the line." Putting his foot in his stirrup, he mounted Bandit and the two started down the hill.

"What do ya figure makes folks like the Ghost, Mr. Hunter. I been thinkin on that one a lot lately. What makes them inta men that can kill like that and feel nuthin?" Stryker looked over to the Hunter. "I mean, he felt nuthin at all…just cut them up with that Bowie a his."

The Hunter thought for a couple minutes before he spoke. "Can't say, Jeff. Seems like some folks get broke somewhere along the way. Somthin snaps in their heads…makes em…different. Makes em dangerous." He reined in and pulled his long glass from his saddlebags. Extending it he looked into the distance. "Appears we're getting closer."

Stryker pulled out his long glass and looked. Collapsing it he looked at the Hunter. "Don't look too concerned do he?" Stryker stood in his stirrups stretching his legs. "Kinda all peaceful like."

The Hunter looked over at Stryker. He was glad Stryker was recognizing things in men now…learning their postures, how they hold themselves in the saddle and how they move about in their daily lives. "Yea, don't appear to have a care does he? Let's give him one, Jeff." The Hunter squeezed Bandit and resumed the tracking of, what they assumed was, Sy Common.

Winding their way through the high desert, the two riders approached the hill they had watched the lone rider go up and over. The trail was rocky and strewn with plant debris, a direct result of a flash flood that had come though a month ago.

As they approached the initial turn to begin the ascent up, a shot rang out from the top. The Hunter and Stryker immediately dismounted, grabbed their rifles and took whatever cover they could find. The shot sounded like a pistol and if it was, they were not in any immediate danger, they were too far down the hill to really be in effective range.

Another shot rang out followed by a voice. "What you want…why you boys following me?" he yelled. "I ain't got nuthin worth nuthin at all."

Stryker listened to the voice until he determined where it was coming from. He motioned over to the Hunter and pointed to a pile of deadfall near the top on the left.

The Hunter adjusted himself, pushing a rock under him away from his body. "What a day," he thought. "We ain't after anything you got mister…so stop shootin at us…Jesus, we just wanna talk is all," he yelled back up the hill.

Stryker lay still and watched the deadfall for movement when he caught the flash of blue go from left to right in a little open area. He laid his Winchester on a dead branch, aimed at the spot and waited.

Some time went by before the man spoke again. The day was getting longer, and the heat was radiating up from the ground where the Hunter and Stryker lay. The breeze wasn't reaching them and the radiant heat was becoming very uncomfortable and making them both surly.

"Look boys, I ain't done nuthin…why you following me at all?"

The Hunter was getting angrier by the minute. "You Sy Common?" he yelled up at the man. "Syrus Common?"

The response was silence again.

Stryker started crawling over to where the Hunter lay. "I can get up there, Mr. Hunter," he fairly whispered. "You fire at that deadfall, hit it a few times, I know I kin get up there him not seein me."

The Hunter thought about it for a moment. "Okay, Jeff, take off on the left there…I'll throw some balls up there, ain't gonna hit him…jest keep his head down," he adjusted his body bringing his Winchester up and levering a cartridge in the chamber. "Ready…go!" He fired a shot then another, making sure he was firing only to appear to be shooting at the deadfall when in actuality he was throwing the balls over the top.

Stryker crouched and made his way up the hill on the left, skirting debris and other deadfall as he went. Nearing the top, he swung wide around some rocks and halted. He could hear the Hunter's shooting and the occasional 'thunk' when a ball hit some wood. He pressed against a rock and peered around the side. He could see the man hunkering down as low as he could to escape the seemingly endless onslaught.

Stryker drew his pistol and yelled to the Hunter "Hold yer fire!" bringing the Colt up at the same time. "Leave it on the ground friend and stand up."

The man looked up at Stryker and his body sagged. Slowly he stood and leaned against the deadfall, letting the debris take his weight. "Aw shit," he said. "Who are you boys anyhow?

"Jest stay there." Stryker went to the edge of the deadfall. "Okay, Mr. Hunter, y'all can come up now," he turned back to the man. "Mr. Hunter asked ya if you was Sy Common, now I'm askin ya…you Sy Common?"

Eastern Men

Finally the man looked up at Stryker. "Yea, I'm Common. Why you boys huntin me?"

It took only a few minutes for the Hunter to come up the hill bringing Waco and the pack mule. "Ya caused us a bunch a problems Mr. Common. I assume that's who you are."

Stryker holstered his pistol and picked up Common's pistol from the ground. "It's him all right. Said so as much." He opened the loading gate turning the cylinder and saw Common was out of ammunition in his pistol. "Pistol's empty too."

"Why are you huntin me?" Common asked now getting frustrated. "I ain't done nuthin!" he yelled.

"According to Dick Gird and Ed Schieffelin ya did, and now, we are gonna take ya back to Contention City…ain't my business to know what ya did or didn't do. It's just my job to find ya, which we done." The Hunter leaned against the end of the deadfall, his left leg starting to ache a little. "Folks call me Hunter and this here, this is Jeff Stryker." He stood back up. "Ain't safe ridin this territory with no cartridges Mr. Common. Ain't safe at all."

"Look, Mr. Hunter, I ain't done nuthin but get accused a stealin dust from Mr. Gird. I ain't stole nuthin from no one," he struggled for words. "They paid me good to keep the dust safe, the gold dust they was takin outta that mine, and it was considerable too," he thought for a minute. "I come ta work one mornin and the office was broke into and the dust gone. I told Mr. Gird and he exploded at me, so I just left until he calmed down," he took a breath. "Next thing I know, the constable's comin after me so I lit out. Didn't take nuthin but my horse and what was in my kit, which weren't much."

"I guess…pretty poor kit you ask me," said Stryker. He walked over to Common's horse and checked him all over. "Needs grain, Mr. Hunter, water and some care on his shoes too…I'll take care of it. Looks ta me though we're gonna be a here at least a day."

"May as well get comfortable Mr. Common." The Hunter went and started unsaddling their mounts, and not being a lot of trees, used two picket pins and lines to stake out all three horses and the mule. When he was done, he dragged his gear over and built a fire pit in the lea of the deadfall. "I'll thank you to inspect that pile there for snakes. Likely to be some in there," he pointed to the deadfall.

"Yea, all right." With a sigh, Common pushed forward off of the deadfall and grabbed a long stick starting from one end of the deadfall to the other he inspected it for snakes and thankfully didn't find any.

Eastern Men

The ride back to Contention City took almost a week, but they finally rode into the front area of the Contention Mine and up to the main building. Dick Gird walked out the front door and greeted the Hunter and Stryker.

"Good to see you, Hunter. Took awhile huh?" Gird stood with his hand on Bandits neck. The Hunter held his hand down and Gird took it. "I have some good news for Mr. Common there." He walked around the Hunter and up to the Horse that Common was riding. "Mr. Common, The person that broke into the office and stole the dust has been caught in Tombstone. His name is Dayton Bartlett and he was an old employee," he felt some embarrassment rising in his face. "I'm sorry to have accused you, Mr. Common, I should have known better and of course your job is still here for you."

Common, reached over and held out his hand to Stryker. "I'll thank you for my pistol Jeff."

Stryker reached into his saddlebags and took out Common's pistol handing it over to him. "Here ya go."

Common took the pistol and shoved it into his pants. "You owe me some money, Mr. Gird, I'll thank you fer it right now."

Eastern Men

"Surely...surely." Gird took out his wallet and handed Common a stack of bills. "A little extra for your troubles Mr. Common."

Common counted out what was owed to him and handed the rest back to Gird. "I ain't taken what ain't rightfully mine, Mr. Gird. Now, I'll be thankin you ta get outta my fuckin way." He moved his horse forward pushing Dick Gird aside. "Mr. Hunter, Stryker...thanks for treatin me proper." Common turned his horse and started off the mine property and headed to wherever he wanted without running.

The Hunter looked at Gird. "You're lucky, Dick, damn lucky."

"For what?" Gird asked as he watched Common leave.

"For him not kickin out yer teeth is what," said the Hunter.

Eastern Men

TWO

"Com'on, Lenny, Jesus, any slower I coulda been doin it myself." Whitey watched Lenny work the buckboard up the steep trail. He finally, in exasperation, went and sat on a large rock just off the trail and waited.

Phineas Bellflower walked over to Whitey, concern written on his face. "Mr. Wellford, what is the holdup? That trail doesn't appear to be that steep and, according to him, Mr. Bristol is a top-notch teamster."

"Aw hell, Mr. Bellflower, Lenny jest gets his britches a might tight every now and again. He don't mean nuthin by it, just sorta happens is all." Whitey picked up his canteen and took a drink just as the buckboard crested the hill and finally made it to a flat spot.

"Fuck, Whitey, ya coulda helped me out there a bit." Lenny jumped off the buckboard and went to check the traces and harness on the two very exhausted horses. When he was satisfied, he went to the wheels and one by one checked spokes, tires and retaining nuts. Finally he stood up pushing his hands into the small of his back and bending backward. "Was there somethin that happened that I didn't know about, Whitey?" he asked.

Eastern Men

"What you talkin about, Lenny?" Whitey stood and brushed off the rear of his trousers. "Ain't nuthin happened."

"I jest thought meybe you was elected President or sumthin...seems it's gettin purty damn hard ta get ya off yer ass these days." Lenny picked up a canteen and took a long drink, a lot of the water missing his mouth and running down his shirt. "These critters need some rest before we move...that okay with you, yer fuckin highness?" he wiped his mouth and mopped his forehead with his sleeve.

Whitey stared at Lenny for a full minute. "Why, Lenny, I'm surprised you would think that way about me...hell we been pards fer the better part a two years now, I ain't ever shirked...far as I know anyhow," he said.

"You ain't never shirked?" Lenny sneered. "Ain't never shirked, I don't reckon ya remember them bandits what robbed us in Mexico then do ya, Whitey?"

"That wasn't shirkin, Lenny, that was plain fuckin runnin...in my book, that's a big difference," said Whitey, starting to get surly about the whole conversation.

"Gentlemen, we have a journey to continue and with you two arguing, it is taking forever to go even two miles," Phineas said. "But, if we are going to stay here..." He went to the buckboard and pulled a wooden folding chair from the back, opened it, set it down, on as flat a spot as he was able, and plopped into it, folding his arms and glaring into the desert vista.

Lenny stared at Bellflower, finally continuing his tirade. "Them sons a bitches took everythin we had…everythin. And you…you high tailed it to the nearest cover you could find…high tailed it and left me standin there with my dick in my hand while them bandits was cleanin us out. You didn't shirk?" he spat. "Well, it sure fuckin looked it ta me. It sure as hell did."

Phineas pulled a flask from his coat pocket and took a big drink before replacing the cap and starting to put it back into his pocket.

Whitey and Lenny stopped their bickering and looked at Bellflower, Whitey running his hand over his mouth and smacking his lips. "Arguin shore makes a feller thirsty Mr. Bellflower," he said. "Develops a powerful thirst it does," said Whitey.

Lenny chimed in. "Sure does sir…we was wonderin if'n y'all would be sharin that flask with us, seeming we're stopped and all?"

Bellflower looked in astonishment at the two men. Just moments before they were in a heated argument and now, they were begging for whiskey. He shook his head in disbelief. "You two finished now, so we can get moving?"

Eastern Men

The two continued to stare at Phineas and at the liquor. After a few minutes, they finally got the hint that there would be no liquor for them right then.

After awhile, when he knew they had cooled down, Lenny watered the team for the buckboard and they waited a little longer before repacking some of the gear Whitey had brought up the hill on his back.

When they were ready, Lenny and Phineas climbed into the buckboard and Whitey mounted his horse and they got back on their way towards Tombstone.

*****

The Hunter turned in the barber's chair staring into the mirror. He had decided to finally shear off his long hair, and now a pile of silver and black hair lay on the floor of the barbershop.

"Ya want me ta trim up that broom ya got on yer lip too, Mister Richmond? That mustache is mighty bushy," the barber asked. "Ain't no trouble."

He thought about it a minute before answering. "I reckon not today, Gus," said the Hunter.

"I don't think he's tasted anythin but whiskers for a considerable long time anyhow," Stryker adjusted himself in the small chair against the wall. " He smiled at his little joke.

Eastern Men

"Looks kinda funny, Mr. Hunter, you not havin any hair and all."

The Hunter glared over at Stryker. "Wouldn't hurt you none to come sit in this chair neither, Mr. Stryker."

Stryker pushed back in his chair and pushed both hands outward. "Nah, I'm purty happy with what I got here on my head, Mr. Hunter." he grinned. "Sides, I got better things ta do today…sleep bein at the top a that list." He got to his feet and stretched. Picking up his hat, he walked to the door and turned around. "I'm goin back down to the gear. You need me, that's where I'll be." He looked at the barber standing by the Hunter and nodded. "Gus."

"Jeff," replied the barber, leaning back down to the Hunter's head. "Let's just clean up this one spot right here…"

Stryker walked down Allen Street in Tombstone. The day was dazzling, as it can be in Arizona and the young man felt fine and happy to be alive. He cut down Fifth Street and turned onto Toughnut, shying away from hotels and boarding houses, they had camped in the same place the Hunter and Jolly had camped so long ago on their hunt for Thomas Hardy.

When he reached their camp, Stryker went to check on the horses and mules. Making sure they were watered with plenty of fodder, he returned to the camp and lay down on his gear.

It was times like these; times when the world slowed and he could catch a breath. Times when he could take and really look at what turns his life had taken. He loved his life now. Of course, he still missed Bobby, and in all likelihood, always would, but it no longer was an ache, it was now more a pleasant memory of a friend now gone. Thinking of Bobby always made him smile as it did now. "Bobby, you would love this life now," he thought. "I ain't never been so free Bobby, never." Slowly he drifted into a calm restful slumber, until the rattlesnake joined him on his blankets.

The movement against his leg caused Stryker to launch himself to his feet pulling his pistol and firing in the breadth of a second. The pistol ball struck the snake directly behind his head and the impact threw the reptile almost four feet from his blankets.

The Hunter stood motionless. He had never seen anyone move that fast in his life, and he had seen plenty of men with speed. He was dumbstruck. He glanced over at the reptile still writhing in his death throes and when he could finally speak, he managed to get out, "I ain't ever seen anyone work a Colt like that, Jeff."

Eastern Men

Stryker spun around to see the Hunter standing there. Holstering his Colt, he knelt back down to his bedding. "I guess that old rattler rattled me some, Mr. Hunter."

"Yea, well don't ever let me rattle you, Jeff," the Hunter said. "I can see what you meant about you and Bobby practicin."

Stryker grinned at him. "Aw hell, Mr. Hunter, I'm jest me is all…nuthin special about it." He sat back on his blankets, thumbed open the loading gate on his Colt and took out the spent cartridge. Laying it aside, he pulled out the remaining cartridges and grabbed his cleaning gear from his saddlebags starting to clean his pistol. "Bobby was better'n me," he finally said.

"Rutan never stood a chance did he?" asked the Hunter. He walked to his gear and sat on his blankets leaning on his saddle. Looking at Stryker carefully he picked up a cup and reaching forward, poured himself some cold coffee. Lying back, he continued to watch Stryker clean his pistol.

Stryker looked over at the Hunter. "Sure he did, Mr. Hunter, everyone has a chance. He coulda not been the way he was." He continued with the cleaning, running the cleaning rod down the barrel.

"Indeed," thought the Hunter. "Indeed."

Eastern Men

THREE

Phineas rolled over on his cot. The morning was cold and as he pulled his blankets higher on his body his thoughts drifting back to the expose' on Michael J. McManus, the fifth ward boss of New York City. The story had blown the lid on one of the most corrupt wards in New York's borough of Brooklyn and had forced Phineas to flee for Chicago with only his life, what little he could carry and the fat check from the New York Republican secreted in his breast pocket. He didn't know if the two gentlemen sent by McManus were still in pursuit or had lost his scent in Chicago, but he sincerely hoped they had. After all, he had left no word on his travels, no hint of his destination. For all they knew, he had been swallowed by Lake Michigan or killed in the back streets of Cicero, which was quickly becoming the home for the multitude of Italian immigrants starting to flood the country.

His brain was ringing the clangor, waking him, and he sat up slowly, taking in all that the Arizona Territory had to offer. He marveled at the deeply purple mountains in the early morning light, the magnificent giant Saguaro cactus that populated the country and the huge variety of birds singing their songs so early in the morning. Glancing to the south, he spotted a roadrunner curiously eyeing something that was managing to keep the bird occupied for some time before Phineas finally broke his gaze and shifted it to the two rascals, Lenny and Whitey rolled in their bedrolls.

"Insolent bastards," he thought. Slowly he made it to a sitting position and then equally as slowly eased himself off of the cot to stretch in the early morning. Busying himself with dressing and his morning rituals, he was paying no attention to either Whitey or Lenny this morning when, in fact, he should have been doing just that.

As Phineas disappeared behind some rocks sporting a box of medicated papers, Lenny and Whitey quickly rose from their blankets dressing hurriedly. Buckling on gun belts and pulling on boots they finally sat at the backend of the wagon and waited for Phineas to finish. For even as black hearted as they pair were, they would never interrupt a man during a nature call.

As Phineas rounded the rocks whistling a vague tune he stopped abruptly in the face of two gun barrels, Whitey and Lennys pistols.

"See here, what's this?" he demanded.

"Well, see, Mr. Bellflower, me n Lenny been thinkin…"

"Yessir we have," chimed in Lenny.

Eastern Men

"And, well, we been thinkin you got so much and we ain't got nuthin." Whitey stood and hitched his trousers then sat back on the end of the wagon. "Seems ta us, you ain't willin ta share and all...well, we jest figured ta take it all." Whitey stopped for a moment before continuing. "Now we ain't got nuthin against ya, Mr. Bellflower, we surely don't...we are jest in need, and well, you got what we need."

"What I have, I have earned, Mr. Wellford, and it isn't for you to remove it from my possession." Phineas stood his ground.

"That's where yer wrong, Mr. Bellflower," Lenny spoke up. "We aim ta take it, and you ain't gonna say shit about it." Lenny holstered his pistol and turned to the wagon taking a length of rope from the back he turned and motioned to Phineas. "Strip that coat, Mr. Bellflower, and the trousers too."

"I most certainly will not..."

The crack of the pistol shot reverberated across the landscape. "Whitey slid forward on the wagon and pointed the pistol barrel directly at Phineas. "Mr. Bellflower, my patience is growing thin and my belly is grumbling. Jest do as Lenny says."

Phineas started stripping off his coat and then his trousers. When he was standing before them in his underwear and shoes, Lenny grabbed him and trussed him arms and legs so even if he could get up, all he could do would be to hop around.

Lying in the dirt, Phineas watched with horror as Lenny and Whitey packed everything and loaded it into the wagon. They left nothing, not even a canteen of water. When they were finished, Whitey turned to Phineas.

"Mr. Bellflower, we thank you fer yer kindness. This gear and wagon will go a long way in helping me and Lenny get across the territory." He knelt to Phineas and spoke softly. "I'm real sorry Mr. Bellflower, but ya shoulda shared."

*****

The shorter of the two men slammed the door in fury, splintering the doorjamb. "Where the fuck could he go?" Spats Melloy leaned against the building for a moment before continuing. "Jesus, Jamie, he's just one fuckin man."

Mister O'Brien sat quietly on a barrel looking at Spats and the closed door. "Mickey, we'll find him. Keep the patience. Mr. McManus said to find him wherever and that's exactly what we are going to do. It's not helping a thing you slamming doors and frightening people. Just relax."

Eastern Men

Spats looked at his friend. "Sorry, Jamie. I just get my rile up. Who woulda thought this rake would be so clever?"

"Mr. McManus sure thought it, Mickey." O'Brien pushed off of the barrel and turned back down the alley. Since arriving in Chicago they had searched all likely hideaways including bordellos on Rush Street and the back streets of Cicero coming up empty. Oh, they got plenty of leads which all turned out to be dead ends. Even the dagos in Cicero were loath to tell them much other than they might have seen him around for a while.

The two men pushed their way through the street teeming with vendors and petty thieves thriving on the one hope that they would all strike it big in the city. That almost never happened. The metropolis of Chicago swallowed up more than a quarter of all that came to live in her walls, either permanently or enough to give some a new start…someone like Phineas Bellflower.

As they reached the corner, Mister O'Brien hailed a hansom and both got aboard. After telling the driver where they wanted to go they settled into the cab. Feeling his anger diffuse, Spats finally spoke.

Eastern Men

"You're right, Jamie. No sense in getting all riled. We'll find him. We found harder ones, we'll find Bellflower."

Mister O'Brien looked over at Spats and nodded. "Now you're thinking, Mickey…now you're thinking."

*****

Phineas Bellflower was in trouble. He had no water, no food, no clothing and no way of protecting himself against, whatever. Trussed like a hog, he couldn't even move his arms enough to get purchase on the ropes binding him. They had done a good job, Lenny and Whitey had. Now he, Phineas, was charged with undoing what Whitey and Lenny had done to him and, at the moment, it appeared it was going to be somewhat hopeless.

Remembering what Whitey and Lenny had said about the critters in the desert, he started flopping like a fool hoping any critters that may have gotten close to him would be disheartened and flee.

Tiring after a few minutes he lay there wondering what in the world he was going to do now. Trying to figure whether this was worse than letting those two thugs, Spats and Mister O'Brien get a hold of him and mulling it over for a few moments, he finally decided it was infinitely better being hogtied in the desert. That decided he set out to determine what was next.

The ropes completely bound him, offering him little movement and even less of an ability to breathe when things got a little too strenuous. Turning his head as far as he could in either direction, he got the same view either way. Unbroken desert as far as his eyes could take him. Bare mesas growing from the desert floor like cathedrals, pockmarked mountains littered with giant rocks and with cactus and mesquite littering the vistas along his line of sight.

"Damn," he thought. "Dammed inconvenient indeed." Rolling on his right side he laid his head on the ground and closed his eyes. The sun was getting fierce and the temperature was growing quickly. But, hour by hour, the day faded into a deep and terrifying blackness.

The night passed slowly as though, on purpose it stalled, leaving him trembling and terrified on the desert floor. When the sun finally did start to rise, he started feeling like maybe he could survive this thing.

Opening his eyes, he saw the creature as it approached slowly, making a jagged trail as it came. It was a scorpion and not any scorpion but a desert bark scorpion. Painful venom and a sting that lasted for days…just the insect that Phineas didn't want to see while bound like a pig. Of course, being from New York, Phineas didn't know all of this, he just knew he didn't want to be around the insect and he rolled in near panic attempting to escape the sting of the insect.

Unfortunately for Phineas, all his struggling put him right in the path of the scorpion and before he knew it, the insect had stung him on his right shoulder before beating a hasty retreat back into the desert.

Panicked now beyond reason, he thrashed about until the pain in his shoulder started becoming worse. He could feel the swelling start and imagined his shoulder and arm turning black, eventually falling off into the sand of the desert. It was then Phineas started with the wailing. Sounding something close to a steer bellowing for a calf, Phineas wailed into the afternoon Arizona sunlight. Sometimes half crying, sometimes half laughing, he bellowed, as he never had before. Grabbing great breaths of air before starting again, he kept at it for a full hour before the pain in his shoulder became something that he had to pay considerable attention.

All of this was for naught, however, as there were no ears to hear him then, just the lonely coyote passing in the morning sun and the hawk circling from above, save the lone

Eastern Men

Apache sitting watching in amusement at the man writhing in the dirt.

*****

The Hunter sat up on his bedroll and looked at Stryker. After that afternoon, there had not been any mention of what the Hunter had seen. There was no need. He was confident of Stryker's abilities and if he wasn't then, he certainly was now.

The sun made slow progress over the Baboquivari Mountains in Pima County. They had decided to take a hunting trip to relax after the hunt for the Ghost. That hunt had taken a lot from Stryker, more than the Hunter even knew. The hunt for the Ghost had made Jeff Stryker who he would be for the rest of his life, had molded and shaped him into a man hunter, a searcher for the lost and missing.

The Hunter reached over and stirred the coals in the fire and leaned over to blow into them hoping to get a flame and he was rewarded with the burst of yellow and orange as the little flame grew and began consuming the wood the Hunter was slowly feeding it. When the blaze was burning brightly he slowly stood, uncurling his bent frame and got the fixings for the morning coffee. When it was cooking by the fire he walked to where they had highlined the horses and mules and grained the eager animals making sure they had plenty of water as well. Taking the time to pat and stroke Bandit, he looked into the mountains around him. Breathing a deep breath of mountain air, he exhaled slowly letting the air escape through his mouth. Reaching up he ran his fingers through his hair, smoothing as he went.

After having been in these mountains and just generally the territory of Arizona as long as he could remember, the territory never failed to make him feel at home. "When god made this land, he must have stopped before he finished," he thought. "But there's enough to make fools like me happy."

The sound of footsteps came up behind him and the Hunter turned to see Jeff Stryker running his hands through his long hair and yawning. "Mornin, Jeff."

"Mr. Hunter," he acknowledged. Stryker walked to Waco and started checking his hooves. "He seemed a little limpy yesterday...thought I better check 'em out this mornin." He finished checking Waco's hooves and stood leaning against the horse. "Sure is purty out here ain't it?"

"It is. A little of every man's soul is out here. Probly what makes it what it is." The Hunter turned back towards the camp. "Coffee's on...you comin?"

Stryker turned back toward the camp, following the Hunter. "You bet."

Eastern Men

After breakfast of biscuits, bacon and coffee the two men packed their mules and saddled their mounts. Turning toward the southeast, they spurred their horses and started their day…headed where, they didn't care. This was their time. No demands, no promises, no hunts to occupy them, nothing in their way but themselves…themselves, and as it turned out, Phineas Bellflower.

FOUR

Phineas tried rolling onto his left side. The swelling and pain were becoming maddening and he knew if he didn't get the weight off of it soon he would, in all probability, scream himself to death.

Glancing up finally, he caught sight of a figure approaching him from his other side. Wiggling like a crazed man he attempted to turn to face his attacker but to no avail, as the man grabbed him and firmly rolled him onto his back.

Phineas' right shoulder shrieked in pain as deft hands untied the bonds and let the rope fall free from his body. He immediately grabbed for his right shoulder and moaned as the intensity of fire again erupted in the sting site.

Looking up he saw an Apache man squatting near him with a very large knife in his hand and Phineas knew this was his last. A look of resignation appeared on Phineas' face as he finally faced death and found it wasn't that scary. "Go ahead," he said. "You may as well just kill me…if you don't I'll just die out here anyway."

The Apache cocked his head as though he didn't understand before speaking. When he finally spoke, Phineas was flabbergasted.

Eastern Men

"I ain't gonna kill ya mister. Least ways I won't if ya stop all that hollerin. It's jest a scorpion sting, ya ain't gonna die." The Apache grabbed Phineas and before he knew, had the tip of the knife in his shoulder, cutting a small hole where the sting was. Taking some herbs from a pouch at his waist, the Apache took a water bottle from his shoulders and wetting the herbs, placed them on the cut. Removing his headband, he tore a small strip from it and wrapped the herbs in place on Phineas' shoulder then sat back and re-wrapped his head. "That oughta do it," he said.

Phineas sat with his mouth hanging open. He never, in all his dreams, figured the savages in this part of Arizona to be proficient in the English language. "You speak English," He finally said in almost a whisper.

"English and Apache...my pa was white ...folks call me The Apache Kid, or just Kid," he said. He looked for a long time at Phineas and taking in the fact that he was dressed in only his underwear and his shoes, the Kid guessed he had been bushwhacked. "Ya ain't gonna last long out here with nuthin but yer underwear mister," he finally said.

*****

The Hunter reined in at the top of a small ridge. It was a little past noon and they were going to stop for the noon break when he spotted two men sitting in a clump of rocks on the far side of a small arroyo. He waited for Stryker to make his way to the top and pointed out the two forms across from them.

"Who do you suppose would be out here like that with nuthin but the air for company?" the Hunter asked Stryker. "This ain't no place to be without."

"Dunno, Mr. Hunter. Seems a bit strange ta me too." Stryker stood in his stirrups and stretched, never breaking his gaze of the two. "Ya know, one a them fellers looks mighty familiar ta me."

The Hunter focused and suddenly it hit him. "It's the Kid," he said. He turned Bandit towards the two men and started the ride down from the ridge.

Ten minutes later Stryker and the Hunter arrived at the rocks where the two men sat. The Kid turned and nodded his acknowledgement that the two men had arrived. Phineas got up and walked to the two horses.

"Thank god you are here sir. This gentleman refuses to talk to me," he jerked his arm towards the Kid.

"Hunter, Stryker," the Kid spoke directly to the two men. "Found this feller here hogtied scorpion stung and layin in the dirt hollerin his fool head off.

"Kid," the Hunter said. "You get anything outta him?"

Eastern Men

"No, he ain't much too talkative and I ain't neither…so we's at a wall, kinda," the Kid said looking at Phineas.

The Hunter took in Phineas sitting there. His underwear torn and his shoes unlaced. The right shoulder on his underwear was cut and bloody from the scorpion sting and the ministrations of the Kid, but other than that, he appeared to be in good shape.

"Who are ya?" the Hunter asked.

Phineas looked up at the Hunter sitting on his horse. He let his gaze move to the young man with him. Both men were dirty, trail dirty, but appeared well fed and well rested and both men sat easily on their horses. He leaned forward to tie his shoes and stood slowly so as not to antagonize the Apache sitting by him.

"Phineas Bellflower at your service," Phineas said. Walking to where the Hunter sat on his horse, he extended his hand.

"From where I sit, don't look like yer exactly at anyone's service, Mr. Bellflower." The Hunter grasped Phineas' hand and the two men shook. "My name is Richmond, but most folks just call me Hunter. This fine young feller on my right goes by the handle a Jeff Stryker."

Eastern Men

Phineas stared for a moment. "Forgive me for staring but a gentleman named Pearly, in Tucson, recommended you quite highly as a guide," he said. Looking down at the earth and over to the Kid still sitting on the rock. "Unfortunately you weren't available and I ended up hiring two nefarious gentlemen named Whitey Wellford and Lenny Bristol."

The Hunter turned and looked at Stryker and within moments the two men were guffawing merrily in their saddles. "You hired the two most worthless men in the territory, Mr. Bellflower," said the Hunter. "In fact, the last time we seen 'em they was hightailin it to the Sea a Cortez." The Hunter stood and swung his leg over the saddle deftly dismounting his horse. Leaning across his saddle, he continued. "Them two came across a fortune and what we hear is they got it all stole by bandits in the mountains. For anyone else, it would be a shame…for them two…they got what they earned."

"Well, they certainly have reaped rewards again, Hunter. I was carrying quite a sum in cash not to mention the supplies." Phineas backed up and sat back down not even caring that the Kid was still there. Heaving a sigh, he put his head in his hands and stared at the ground.

"That's what he's been doin…jest sittin there with his head down. I told him not ta worry but, he ain't listenin ta me," said the Kid standing and stretching. "We should probly get him some drawers Hunter."

Eastern Men

FIVE

The dust was relentless. It flew in the windows of the jostling coach in great clouds settling on and in everywhere and everything. The bouncing and constant rolling was making the two eastern men seasick and they prayed silently that the coach would stop soon.

"Try looking at the horizon," said a woman sitting across from them. "I find it helps keep your lunch down."

Spats looked at the woman. She was plain, in a farmer sort of way and somewhat portly from what he could tell with her sitting, he decided. "Thanks lady, I'll try it," he responded. Turning his head toward the window, he fixed his stare on a far point and kept it there and in a short while, his stomach started feeling better.

Turning to his right, he elbowed Mr. O'Brien. "Jamie, did ya hear what the lady said?"

Coming out of a slumber, Mr. O'Brien turned to look at Spats with some disgust. "You just woke me up Mickey…what the hell you want?" He crossed his arms across his chest and closed his eyes again.

"I guess nuttin," Spats said. "Just tryin ta help yous out is all."

Eastern Men

Mr. O'Brien opened his eyes again and looked at Spats. "Look Mickey, leave me be…my stomach is all in knots."

"That's what I was gonna tell ya, Jamie. This lady told me ta stare at the horizon and it works." Spats shrunk back into his seat again staring out the window.

Mr. O'Brien sat up and looked to his right out the open window at a mesa in the distance. Presently, his stomach stopped the churning and the dizziness eased. "I'll be damned," he thought. "This fuckin works."

*****

Lenny went through the last of Phineas' trunks and sat back. "I swear, Whitey, if that Mr. Bellflower had any money in here, I'll be dammed if I kin find it."

Whitey took another drink from the flask of whiskey. "You know he had money, Lenny, now we just gotta be smarter than Mr. Phineas fuckin Bellflower."

Lenny sat back on his heels sighing an exasperated sigh. "Well hell, Whitey, I'll start lookin agin…gotta be here in this shit." Lenny got to his knees and started crawling to the first of the open trunks. Clothing was strewn everywhere and he pushed it aside angrily as he made his way to the chest. Arriving on his hands and knees, he pulled the trunk closer to himself and started a thorough investigation of the luggage. Ripping the lining and dismantling the piece, he soon gave up and moved to the second one. Again, he tore the lining out and fairly tore the trunk apart before moving to the third and final piece.

Lenny sat down cross-legged and stared hard at the trunk before pulling it to him. Methodically ripping and pulling the lining out, his fingers happened to engage a small spring catch on the upper inside corner and the entire bottom of the chest sprang open. Lenny stared with eyes wide open and finally was able to speak. "W…Whitey, you gotta see this…there must be thousands in here…thousands I tells ya!" He reached into the compartment and withdrew a stack of bills. "Look a this Whitey! That fuckin Bellflower was loaded!"

Whitey jumped to his feet and scurried to where Lenny sat with the chest open. Peering in, he almost started drooling at the abundant cash that had been hiding in the chest. Lenny was right, there must be thousands in there and it was all theirs…all of it.

Whitey tapped Lenny on the shoulder with the flask. "Here ya go," said Whitey. Then he looked down and the reality of it hit him. "Holy shit Lenny, how much ya think…we's fuckin rich agin is what it looks like ta me and this time there ain't no fuckin Mesican bandits lurkin about."

Eastern Men

"Nope and no fuckin Phineas Bellflower neither," Lenny said.

An hour later the two men had all the useable stores packed on one of the extra horses and were riding away leaving the majority of items belonging to Phineas Bellflower scattered and blowing across the desert floor. They had virtually taken everything of value including a very expensive gold Waltham hunter case pocket watch and the final tally in cash of over thirty thousand dollars. They were rich all right, but then, they had been rich before. These two, Whitey Wellford and Lenny Bristol, just seemed to have a problem with holding on to anything they had earned, stole or misappropriated.

*****

Stryker rummaged through the packs until he found an extra pair of trousers and bandana. Tossing the trousers to Phineas, he waited until Phineas had slipped them on before showing him how to wet and tie the bandana on his head Mexican peasant style.

When he was done with Phineas, Stryker walked back to where the Hunter sat waiting. "Well, Mr. Hunter, appears as though we have Mr. Bellflower here about as ready as he can get considerin he ain't got nuthin left a his own anyhow." He squatted down next to the Hunter. "Can't say how excited he's gonna be ridin atop that durn mule a yers though…that could be jest plain embarrasin."

The Hunter glanced over at Phineas standing near the mule in poorly fitting trousers, underwear, shoes and a blue bandana tied around his head. The Hunter couldn't help but grin at the thought of Phineas perched on top of his mule. Turning back to Stryker, he wiped some sweat from his neck and spoke. "Appears Mr. Phineas Bellflower is gonna have one hell of a story to tell when we get him down to Tombstone eh Jeff?" He stood slowly, letting his body unravel on it's own, hocked and spat in the dirt. "I figure about three days from here to Tombstone, or, two days to catch those two…" he stopped, thinking of what to call them. "Those two morons."

"I'm thinkin," said Stryker. "Let's go after Whitey and Lenny."

"I'm thinkin the same thing Jeff," said the Hunter. "They left good enough tracks with that wagon and all…should be able to come right up on 'em easy." He pulled his hat off and scratched his head. "I sure hope old Phineas there don't do a pile a hollerin on that mule."

Stryker smiled at the Hunter and walked over to Waco tightening his cinch and adjusting his gear, he finally went to Phineas and assisted him with getting on the Hunter's pack mule then mounted his horse, took up the lead for his mule and sat comfortably waiting for the Hunter.

The Kid, who had been watching all of this stoically, finally got up and walked to his horse leading him back to the little group. Mounting, he turned towards the Hunter. "Hunter, you watch yer back...I heard some more warriors are fixin ta jump San Carlos agin...maybe, maybe not, but anyhow, ya jest watch yerself." He gathered his reins and nodded towards Stryker. "Stryker." With that, he turned his horse and started for the northeast and the New Mexico territory.

The Hunter and Stryker watched him ride away. Phineas was looking very uneasy sitting atop the mule and Stryker sidled his horse over to him.

"Easy Mr. Bellflower. Fussin around up there is more likely ta make him angry than make you more comfy," Stryker said. "You don't want no angry mule under ya neither."

"Mr. Stryker, something seems to be poking me in my posterior" said Phineas. "It's sharp and it's hard."

"It's sharp indeed Mr. Bellflower, it's my Sharps rifle," said the Hunter. "Hop down, we'll fix 'er for ya...easy now, don't go spookin that mule."

Eastern Men

The Hunter loosened the ropes and repositioned the rifle so the hammer wouldn't be poking Phineas and retied everything. "There ya go Mr. Bellflower. Up ya go." He assisted Phineas in remounting the mule.

"Much better Mr. Hunter, thank you," said Phineas.

"Jeff, you take the lead, I'll hang back with Mr. Bellflower here," said the Hunter as he mounted his horse.

"On my way Mr. Hunter," said Stryker. He squeezed Waco and rode off following the wagon tracks that led directly north towards the San Carlos Apache reservation.

*****

The stagecoach pulled to a stop in front of the Wells Fargo station in Tucson and a handful of dusty, thirsty, irritable people stepped off. Spats and Mr. O'Brien waited for the driver to toss down their luggage and as he had with Phineas Bellflower, aimed for the derby hat worn by Spats Melloy. Spats looked up in time and ducked as the bag thumped to the street. In a flash Spats was on the stage and pulled the driver over the side to a heap in the dirt.

"Ya think yous funny fella?" Spats sneered. "Yous don't look so almighty rollicky right now." He picked up his bag and turned to the stationmaster. "Where's the nearest bar?"

Eastern Men

Bob Paul strode across the street. He had seen Spats pull the driver over the top of the coach and he elbowed his way in front of the stationmaster. "Hello gents," He said.

Spats looked over at Paul and saw a tall portly man well over two hundred pounds. He was wearing an ill-fitting suit and a hat rakish on his head. Facial whiskers filled out the picture, coupled with a booming voice; they were looking at Bob Paul, Pima County Sheriff.

"Fella threw my bag at me," said Spats. He stared at the sheriff. "Ain't no one gonna throw my bags at me sheriff…no one."

Paul looked at Spats and Mr. O'Brien. "Where you boys from?" he asked.

Mr. O'Brien, becoming irritated at the delay, answered sharply. "Brooklyn, New York, and unless you have some reason to delay us, we'll be on our way."

"You boys understand one thing," Paul said. We don't take to roughhousin or hard boiled shenanigans in Pima county from no one…you understand."

Mr. O'Brien looked at Paul and then to Spats. "Yes sheriff, we understand. Now, would you be so kind as to direct us to the nearest bar and we'll be on our way."

"Right down the street here. The Arizona Metro…clean and Pearly don't overcharge," Paul said.

Eastern Men

"Then we'll be going. Afternoon Sheriff." Mr. O'Brien motioned for Spats and the two men turned and headed to the Metro for a cold beer and more, they wanted information about one, Phineas Bellflower.

Bob Paul watched them go. "Those two are hard cases," he thought. "I wonder what they're doin here?" He turned and walked back across the street to resume his afternoon in the chair right outside his office.

Eastern Men

SIX

Spats and Mr. O'Brien walked into the Metro and straight to the bar. Setting their bags on the floor, Spats started knocking on the bar, trying to get the bartenders attention. When finally the bartender turned around and noticed them, he walked over to them and placing his hands on the bar, the bartender spoke. "Gentlemen, what can I get ya?"

Mr. O'Brien was the first to answer. "A beer and a glass of Scotch," he said.

"Now ain't that funny. A feller was in here last week looking for scotch whiskey too, and I told him just what I'm gonna tell you...ain't no scotch, we got rye, bourbon or Irish," the bartender said.

Mr. O'Brien looked at Spats then back to the bartender. "Irish and can you recall this gent's name?" he asked.

"The bartender scratched his head for a moment thinking of the mans name when it suddenly hit him and he snapped his fingers. "Funny sort a name...Phineas I think. Yea, that's it, Phineas Bellflower." He looked over to Spats. "And you, what can I get you?"

Eastern Men

Spats looked at the bartender. "Same as him make my whiskey bourbon though."

"Say friend, you gotta name?" Mr. O'Brien leaned on the bar as the bartender was getting their drinks.

"Pearly. Just plain Pearly," came the reply.

"Well, just plain Pearly, any idea where this gent went?" asked Mr. O'Brien.

"Well, I ain't sure…you got a name mister?" asked Pearly.

"Mr. O'Brien," came the answer.

"Christian name?" asked Pearly as he sat the drinks in front of the men.

"Mister," said Mr. O'Brien. "And, I'll be asking you again, just plain Pearly, do you know where he went?"

Pearly stood transfixed for a moment. His head told him these men were hard men and would do anything to get answers. "All I know is he hired two bounty hunters named Whitey and Lenny to guide him to Tombstone and they left last week." He pulled the bar towel from his shoulder and wiped his hands nervously.

"Now that wasn't so bad was it?" Mr. O'Brien stood up straight, drank the whiskey in one gulp, drank half the beer and nudged his companion. "Come on, Spats, let's see if we can get an idea where exactly he went."

Eastern Men

Spats finished his whiskey and beer and the two men gathered their bags and walked out the door in search of Phineas Bellflower's trail.

*****

The Hunter called a halt and handed a canteen to Phineas. "Mr. Bellflower, pull the bandana off and pour some water on it before putting it back on yer head." He watched Phineas re-wet the bandana and tie it back onto his head before taking a big drink for himself then handing the canteen back to the Hunter.

"Thank you, Hunter. That was refreshing," said Phineas. He looked up and saw a lone figure coming in at a trot. "I do believe that is master Stryker."

The Hunter looked up just as Jeff Stryker was riding up to them.

"I found where they stopped, Mr. Hunter. Found a lot of Mr. Bellflower's things too…sorta scattered like all over the desert. Trunks all tore up and thrown about," said Stryker. "I piled a lot of it together in one a the trunks that wasn't tore up too bad."

"They leave the wagon too?" asked the Hunter.

"Yessir, banged it up pretty good before they left though. Ain't much good ta no one now," Stryker answered.

"No stores neither, other than what they dumped on the ground."

Phineas looked in the direction of their travel. All that was visible to him were the mountains in the distance, the mesas jutting from the desert floor and the interminable cactus that was everywhere. What he didn't see, or care to see, was the life that abounded in Arizona. The cactus flowers hidden in the folds of the cactus, the abundant rabbits, snakes, lizards and insects…the mule deer and the bighorn sheep on the sides of the mountains. These were all things the Hunter and Stryker saw and appreciated. Phineas could only see his discomfort and it shielded his eyes from the beauty that was the Arizona territory.

"How far out Mr. Stryker?" Phineas asked in exasperation.

Stryker looked at Phineas. Saw the discomfort and the pleading in his eyes. "Half a day at the most Mr. Bellflower." Stryker dismounted and tightened Waco's cinch. Took his canteen from his saddle and took a large drink. "Spring about ten miles out." He looked at the Hunter. "Cold and clear. Maybe Mr. Bellflower can get washed up some…seein as how it appears he don't like bein dirty so much." He knelt down and let some dirt fall through his fingers. "Hell, meybe we can all get washed up some…we're all gettin a bit ripe." He stood and remounted his horse.

"Good Idea Jeff." The Hunter turned to Phineas. "Mr. Bellflower, Jeff says there's a nice cold spring about ten miles up, in case you didn't hear."

"I heard him Hunter and it sounds wonderful," said Phineas. He swept his arm in front of him in a mock grandiose fashion. "I swear, I don't know how you men live out here. It's just so…It's just so empty."

The Hunter squeezed Bandit and started moving forward. "Well see Mr. Bellflower, if ya really look, it ain't so empty at all." He pointed to a rocky outcropping to the northwest of them. "If ya look on that ridge, there are about 6 bighorn sheep grazing up there. See, ain't so empty, there's somethin everywhere if ya jest take the time to find it."

"I suppose I have spent so much time in the noise and bustle of the cities, I never took the time to look around in the quiet times." Phineas adjusted on the packs. "You men seem to relish the living out here, and me, well me, I would rather be in a city or big town that offers diversions besides counting stars at night. I suppose I am doomed to being an eastern city man."

*****

Eastern Men

Mr. O'Brien counted out the money and handed it to the owner of the livery. "There you have it, two hundred and fifty dollars. Are you sure we have everything now?" he asked.

"Are you sure you know where yer goin? This here is Arizona, not Boston," said the liveryman.

"Brooklyn," said Mr. O'Brien.

"Brooklyn, Boston, don't matter none. This here is Arizona. Out here just the fuckin country will kill ya." The liveryman started to turn and stopped. Turning back to Mr. O'Brien, he said, "A little advice for ya friend. You're out there and it gets quiet. I mean real quiet like there ain't even any fuckin birds chirpin…ya best get yer ass down, cause it's probly 'paches."

"Apache Indians?" asked Spats.

"Yea, Apache Indians and right now army's got em all stirred up," the liveryman scratched his beard. "Like I said, it gets real quiet, get yer asses down." He turned and walked into his room closing the door after himself.

Spats walked to the pack mule and inspected it again for tight cinches, the liveryman had shown him how to adjust the breeching and breast collar and he did that again now. Standing up, he walked to Mr. O'Brien. "Jamie, we're as ready as we are ever gonna be." He walked over to his horse, put his foot into the stirrup and attempted to mount the horse, but instead, the saddle rolled over to the side then underneath the horse and the horse commenced bucking and spinning. On one spin the horse bucked and kicked the side of the building, bringing the liveryman back outside in a hurry.

Grabbing the flailing lead, he got the horse to stop long enough to get the saddle off and calm him down. "What the fuck did you do? Try to get on the fuckin horse with a loose cinch?"

Spats stood rubbing his shoulder, the one the horse had slammed into on one of the bucking spins. "Yea, yous might say that."

*****

Whitey reined in his horse. Standing in his stirrups he surveyed the landscape in front of them. "I'm getting so's I hate the fuckin desert, Lenny, I truly am," Whitey said. "Every fuckin mile is jest like the last fuckin mile."

"Yea, ain't a lot a difference tween this hill and that hill is there?" commented Lenny. Scratching his head he looked around "You even know where the fuck we are, Whitey?"

"Last I checked, we was in Arizona Territory, Lenny...fuck if I know where we're at now," said Whitey.

Eastern Men

Lenny pondered for a minute. "Meybe we'll get lucky and still be in Arizona."

"A course we're still in Arizona, shitbird. We ain't been ridin more'n a couple two, three days," replied Whitey. "Sides, ain't there a marker or sumthin if we leave Arizona?"

"Well, I hope it ain't no sign," said Lenny. "I cain't be reading no sign...hurts my eyes."

"What're you talking about, Lenny? You read that paper on that asshole the Ghost."

"Yea, well that was differnt, it was small and my eyes could see all of it at the same time...signs are differnt, I gotta move my eyes over 'em...gives me a sightful headache," said Lenny.

"What time ya got, Lenny?" Whitey adjusted in his saddle. "I'm gettin hungry."

"Yer gettin hungry? What time I got? Fuck Whitey, ya jest called me a shitbird...now ya want somethin too? Yer an asshole ya know that?" Lenny pulled Phineas' pocket watch from his pocket and flipped it open. "Four-thirty," he said.

"Well, hell, no wonder I'm hungry, we ain't et since six this mornin." Whitey looked around. "Looks ta be a good place ta camp down that draw to them cottonwoods there." He pointed them out to Lenny.

Eastern Men

"Looks ta be all right," said Lenny. He settled back into his saddle and followed Whitey down into the draw to the cottonwoods rustling in the afternoon breeze.

By late evening the two men had taken care of their animals, cooked and eaten their supper and were no laying on their bedrolls drinking whiskey and trying to figure out what they were going to do with their newfound wealth, and how they were going to get out of the territory with it without being caught again.

Eastern Men

SEVEN

Two and a half hours later the three men reached the spring. As Stryker had promised, it was cold clear water and they wasted no time in stripping down and refreshing themselves in the early afternoon sun. When they were finished, they saddled their mounts and rode off to the final resting place of Phineas' worldly possessions.

When they rode up to the area where Stryker had found Phineas' gear, Stryker's description was, to the trained eye, somewhat edited. The area was strewn with castoff goods and trash. Phineas' clothing was indeed stacked on one of the trunks but the rest of his gear was just plain unusable. The wagon was able to provide enough wood for firewood. Phineas' clothes, although most were stacked, and what possessions were left, were scattered and it took the men a little more than a quarter hour to gather them and dress Phineas in his own clothing.
After dressing, Phineas walked to the trunks, torn apart by Whitey and Lenny. Looking at the trunk that had held his money, he sat down hard on a rock and stared.

Turning to the Hunter, Phineas was almost in tears. "They took it all, Hunter, everything I had of value in this world either monetarily or by sentiment." He took a deep breath and continued. "I should have listened to the stable master…he told me not to trust those two. He warned me more than once while we were settling up for the wagon and the team."

"Mr. Bellflower, don't help much ta be thinkin hard on this. Just know you have learned somethin here. Somethin you'll likely take with you from now on," said Stryker. "I made my share of mistakes in my life. Lord knows, but he allowed me ta live and learn from em too…that's the pure truth of it, Mr. Bellflower, it truly is."

The Hunter looked at Stryker. Those words were the most he had ever heard him say at one time. Starting a big grin, he looked back over at Phineas. "Sides, ya got me and Jeff here, Mr. Bellflower. Ya coulda done worse." Glancing at Stryker he grinned even larger. "Then again, maybe not," he said.

Stryker grinned too. "Yessir, you sure coulda." And he looked at the Hunter.

The Hunter and Stryker were taking care of the horses and looking at the debris left by Whitey and Lenny. The Hunter shook his head in disgust. "You'd think a feller could bury his own garbage," he said kicking it into a pile so they could bury it in the morning with their own. "These two are really getting under my skin Jeff. They ain't thinkin and they are wasteful."

Stryker finished watering the horses and mule. Picking up a can, he tossed it onto the pile. "Won't be long, Mr. Hunter, when everywhere ya look someone's gonna leave his leavins layin out. Seems like every camp we go to anymore, someone's left stuff thrown about."

"Seems that way don't it," said the Hunter. "Well, let's get some supper in us. We gotta get early in the morning if we are ta catch up with them scoundrels."

"Yessir, be right there," said Stryker. He leaned over and adjusted the lead on Waco to make sure he wouldn't catch up in it during the night then turned and walked back to camp. "Tomorrow's gonna be an interesting day," he thought. "Yessir, real interesting indeed."

By seven o'clock all three men were in their blankets and by themselves in the gathering darkness. All had thoughts, all had ambitions and lives they wanted to live out. The quiet was a welcome respite from the day and all three took advantage of the solace it brought with it. One by one they drifted into sleep with the Hunter and Stryker keeping an ear on the stock.

Eastern Men

Phineas stirred in his blankets. He didn't much like sleeping on the ground, it caused his muscles to shriek and the pain could be found everywhere on him. He sat up and looked around, he expected to see two sleeping men and what he saw was horses saddled, mule packed and the remnants of breakfast in a pan by the fire. Stryker was by the horses burying their leavins and Whitey and Lenny's debris while the Hunter squatted by the fire staring at him.

"Well sir, I can't say as I quite expected this at all," said Phineas. "I dare say you two were up rather early."

"Get enough sleep there, Mr. Bellflower?" asked the Hunter.

"Quite...quite. A bit dicey sleeping on the desert floor, but with everything it isn't, it is a far better alternative then I had, Hunter," Phineas said.

"Like I told ya yesterday, Mr. Bellflower, things in the desert aren't always like ya see em," said the Hunter. "Keep yer eyes and ears open. You'll learn, or you'll die...there just ain't no other options." He turned to what was left of the fire and poured Phineas a cup of coffee. Handing it to Phineas he continued. "Drink up, we got a long day today."

*****

Eastern Men

Sy Common was packing his gear, making ready to leave the area he had stayed in for the past three days when the first rifle ball plowed into his packs. Immediately reaching for his Winchester, he sought cover. He didn't know what he was facing, but whatever, or whoever, it was, was shooting at him. Working the lever on his rifle he scanned the area in front of him as best he could when the second ball, and then the fusillade, resounded, kicking chips of rock and debris into the air and into his face. Common hunkered down as low as he could get to escape the rifle balls whining in the air and impacting all around where he lay.

From his vantage point he could see the valley floor and the surrounding craggy rock formations forming a semi-circle around him. He guessed, by the volume of the fire, that whoever it was, was hidden and firing from the rocks around him and that there were more than just a couple. "It's gonna be a long day," he thought as he tried to decide if he was brave enough to scramble for his canteen on his packs. That is, until a ball slammed into the canteen and he watched as the water drooled out and made a puddle below in the sand. "Shit!" he screamed out loud. "It really is gonna be a long fuckin day," he said to himself.

Eastern Men

An Apache warrior peered over the edge of rocks at the huddling man in front of him. Bringing his rifle up he sighted down the barrel and fired. The rifle ball impacted directly in front of Common's foot causing him to jerk it back. The Apache immediately moved to a different position and fired again but his rifle misfired jamming the cartridge in the breech. His rifle was a Springfield Trapdoor cavalry carbine and the models were known to have misfire and jamming problems, now being a perfect example. The Apache pulled his knife and flipping up the trapdoor on the carbine, furiously trying to get the cartridge loosened from the rifle.

As he worked on the jammed rifle, three other Apaches were working their way lower to the huddling man. Halfway down in the rocks, they heard a whistle and looked up. On the top of the ridge, they saw two more warriors flailing a blanket in the air and pointing towards the valley floor. There they saw three riders almost a mile away but coming fast.

The three Apaches stopped their descent, and watched the riders approaching then come to a halt. Presently two came on at a gallop and one stayed back. A little confused, the three Apaches again started their descent.

Eastern Men

Stryker had heard the gunfire erupt and had galloped back from his scout to Phineas and the Hunter. When he got back to them, almost a mile distance, he reined in Waco and swung the horse around facing the direction of the gunfire. "A lot of shootin up there Mr. Hunter. I can make out six, eight rifles."

"Let's go!" yelled the Hunter. All three men urged their mounts into a gallop. The Hunter and Stryker were pulling far out in front of Phineas, as he was still perched atop the packs and experiencing the ride of his life, bouncing and rolling as the mule ran headlong after the Hunter and Stryker. Stryker had dropped the lead to his mule and the mule was loose and running with the rest but staying close to the big white mule Phineas was riding.

Finally pulling up, the Hunter turned to Phineas. "Stay here Mr. Bellflower. I mean it, no matter, you stay here," the Hunter said.

"Happily Hunter. My bottom is getting all worn down on top of those infernal packs," he said. "Besides, I have no knowledge of the correct side of a weapon other than a fencing epee," he added.

"A what?" asked the Hunter and then he shook his head. "Never mind, you jest stay here is all." He spun Bandit and he and Stryker charged up the hill to the rocks where Sy Common was fighting for his life.

Phineas watched them go and breathed a sigh of relief. Adjusting himself on the packs he looked up the hill where, presently, there was sporadic very heavy gunfire. Settling down atop the mule, he relaxed and waited.

Stryker reached Common first and pulling his Winchester, he leapt from Waco on the run and went skidding into Sy Common, finally grinding to a halt against his leg. Turning quickly he saw the Hunter pulling his Winchester and dismounting, rushing to another spot for cover. Opening fire at the rocks above them, the three men managed to keep the incoming volume of fire down and soon they settled in and started placing their shots at known targets. The firing, although constant, ebbed and flowed in a deadly dance meant for death of one or all three men in the small clearing as the rifle balls whizzed by like bees or impacted rocks and dirt with deadly thuds or whining off into the distance.

"Seems ta me, ya got a bad habit a getting yerself into messes Sy," said Stryker as he jacked another cartridge into his Winchester and fired at movement to his left.

Eastern Men

"Where the fuck you boys come from Jeff? I mean I look up and you and Mr. Hunter are chargin up that damn hill like the cavalry," said Common. "I ain't complainin mind ya…you boys are surely a sight all right."

"You okay Common?" yelled the Hunter.

"Yessir, a little shook is all, but this time I got cartridges," answered Common, grinning broadly. "They hit my canteen though and by the looks of it, my water bladders too." Common took a deep breath and turned snapping a shot up the rocks."

"Anyone see em?" asked the Hunter. He leaned against a rock and reloaded his rifle. "Them's Apaches all most sure," he said. "They want the horse and mule and anything else ya got they can use." The Hunter called to Stryker. "They's probly the ones the Kid told us about Jeff."

"Yessir, I already figured." Stryker rose and fired three shots up into the rocks. Ducking back down, he quickly reloaded his rifle.

Sy Common rose, took aim and fired with the result an Apache tumbling from the rocks and landing face down on the hard packed dirt with a thud. In the ensuing moments, everything got quiet. The men waited, barely breathing, expecting a rush any moment, the acrid gun smoke slowly dissipating in the slight breeze just starting in the canyon.

Eastern Men

After ten minutes, the Hunter rose and walked to the Apache body lying by the packs on the ground. "They've quit the fight," he said. "There's probly a couple more shot up in them rocks, and we're just gonna leave em there for their friends ta get I think." The Hunter rolled over the dead Apache and started going through his body. On it he found a pocket watch, a cartridge belt with 45.70 ammunition, a Colt pistol around his waist and a large sheathed hunting knife.

Stryker watched the Hunter go through the Apache's things. "Looks like some poor soul probly lost his kit to this one," he said. He turned to gather the horses and saw an amazing sight. There, coming up the hill full speed, was Phineas Bellflower astride the Hunter's white mule.

Phineas listened to the battle raging for a full ten minutes when his eyes caught sight of two figures cresting a hill, obviously purposely staying far away from the fighting. He immediately recognized the two men as Whitey Wellford and Lenny Bristol and found they were within hailing distance. He cupped his hands over his mouth and yelled. "Hold Mr. Wellford, I would like a word with you."

The response was immediate and loud. Both Whitey and Lenny drew their revolvers and began firing at Phineas, puffs of white smoke preceding the crack of the shot. Pistol balls began falling around him and Phineas turned the mule as best he could and got the mule into a run towards the hill and safety. Probable safety at least as there was still sporadic shots coming from the hill.

Stryker turned and saw Phineas running pell mell up the hill and yelled over to the Hunter. "Mr. Hunter, look!" he said.

The Hunter stood up just as Phineas was cresting the hill and one last shot echoed from the ridge. The mule screamed and turned sideways, stretching and turning its head as it dropped to its left side spewing Phineas and supplies everywhere.

"Jesus Christ Mr. Bellflower, when I tell you ta stay put, that's what I fuckin mean, stay the fuck put! That's my favorite fuckin mule damn you," the Hunter yelled. He walked over to the mule and could see he was dead, shot through the head. Squatting down he patted the mule's head and stood. "This is just fuckin great." He said.

"I had to Hunter," said Phineas feeling somewhat embarrassed.

"Yea, yea why'd ya have to Mr. Bellflower?" asked the Hunter sarcastically.

"Because Whitey Wellford and Lenny Bristol were shooting at me," answered Phineas and he sat heavily on a rock, putting his head in his hands.

*****

"Oh shit, Whitey, that was Mr. Bellflower!" said Lenny re-holstering his big Remington pistol. "Where the fuck did he come from?"

"Aw fuck, Lenny, I'll bet he's with that Richmond asshole. We seen that big white mule in Mexico, remember?" asked Whitey.

"Them 'paches we seen a ways back musta jumped someone up there then. Let's get while we still can, Whitey. The idea of havin ta deal with that Hunter feller again don't sit too comfy in my guts," said Lenny. "Sides, if ya remember, we got a whole passel a Mr. Bellflower's shit."

Whitey turned his horse east. Spurring him viciously, the two men rode as quickly as they could to the east hoping to put a considerable amount of distance between the Hunter, Stryker, Phineas Bellflower and now, Sy Common.

*****

Spats got up stretching his torso. Sleeping on the ground was not agreeable to his body, having had a bed to sleep in every night in Brooklyn, so every morning for the past three mornings he had gotten up having to stretch the kinks out. He wasn't sure which was worse. Sleeping on the ground with all the delightful critters of the desert or riding that infernal horse for hours at a time, not really sure where they were going. Finally able to move without stumbling, he walked over to the sleeping figure of Mr. O'Brien.

"Rise and shine, Jamey…another beautiful fuckin day in…I don't know, Arizona," said Spats. "Another couple a days and my ass is gonna be flatter than a spatula."

Mr. O'Brien rolled over and cocked one eye at Spats. "Is it complainin your gonna be doin this mornin, Mickey?" He managed to get into a sitting position. "Because if it is, I am just gonna leave you here and you can walk the fuck back for all I care." Getting to his knees, Mr. O'Brien staggered to his feet and stretched. "Or I'll just shoot you."

Spats looked at Mr. O'Brien. "You ain't gonna shoot me Jamie. I know better. Besides, the boss wouldn't be happy, and we don't want to make Mr. McManus unhappy…hell he might just feel it necessary to send us after…us." Spats walked back to his bedroll and began rolling it back up when a little scorpion scurried out from underneath. Spats jumped back exclaiming. "Fuck! Little shit coulda had me, Jamie."

Mr. O'Brien shook his head. "Mickey, grow up. We're here for a reason, not because we want to be. Keep rememberin that with all your other troubles, Mickey. And, I might say, all your whinin is doing nothin for the general temperance of this camp." Mr. O'Brien walked a short distance away to relieve himself. Returning to the camp he busied himself with packing up their stores in the panniers.

Spats watched him for a moment before he walked off for his morning relief.

An hour later the two men were in the saddle heading in a general easterly direction. Spats was miserable. He was saddle sore and his legs felt like they were on fire. Coupled with the pain in his lower back, he was as unhappy as he ever remembered being, yet, he had vowed not to say anything to Mr. O'Brien causing another reaction like he got that morning.

The day passed slowly and midday came two days later, or so it felt to Spats' hind end. By the time they stopped for their noon meal, Spats was so glad to get off his horse he almost cried in relief.

Mr. O'Brien dismounted and pulled the saddle from his horse and the packs from the mule, unsaddling it as well. When he had finished watering the stock, he built a small fire and started some coffee. Waiting for the coffee to cook, he looked out across the desert.

Eastern Men

"Nothin out there, Mickey, nothin but dead shit and rocks. How the hell do people find people out here? It isn't natural. Not at all," said Mr. O'Brien. Pulling his bowler from his head and giving it a good solid scratch, he thought for a moment then spoke. "You know, if we were the smart of it, we would be goin to a place where we know that asshole, Bellflower, is gonna show up, and just sit and wait for him." He picked up a small twig and poked into the dirt. "Didn't that bartender, just plain Pearly, say Tombstone was southeast? Why don't we go there?"

Spats looked at Mr. O'Brien. "Any more time on that horse than is necessary, and my fundament is gonna be blistered raw," he thought. "Yea sure, Jamie, let's fuckin head for Tombstone, can't be that far…can it?" he said.

After coffee and an hour resting the animals, the two were again in the saddle and changing their direction to south. Mr. O'Brien looked at a map and pulling a compass from his kit, figured out a general direction of travel. From where he figured they were to the town of Tombstone, by his reckoning, was still over sixty miles of rugged Arizona desert.

Spats sat stoically on his horse watching Mr. O'Brien. "Sixty fuckin miles," he thought. "Great, only sixty more fucking miles. May as well just cut my ass off now," he mumbled to himself.

Eastern Men

EIGHT

Lenny walked back to their camp and sat heavily on a rock. Looking at Whitey, he moved his knife blade deftly over the small piece of wood he was holding. As the wood got smaller, Lenny got more agitated and finally spewed his thoughts. "Ya know, that fuckin Richmond and that asshole Stryker catch us they're gonna peel our skin off like potatoes." He had stopped whittling but started again with a vengeance. "Yessir, we're gonna be in a heap a shit and there ain't no way we kin take those two...probly not even a ways out with our Winchesters."

Whitey looked at Lenny furiously shaving the wood with his knife. "What are ya makin, Lenny?"

"Fuckin splinters, Whitey, what's it look like I'm makin...Jesus fuckin Christ...you blind too?" said Lenny. "Now, hows about addressin the pressin fuckin problem we got here, Whitey."

"I don't see no problem, Lenny, none at all...far as I kin guess is they are gonna be so busy tryin ta get mounts for everyone they won't be even two-three days back. Plenty a time ta get the fuck outta here," said Whitey. "Sides, it needs ta be, we jest set up an ambush and take them close in."

91

Eastern Men

"Yea like we took that kid, Stryker, before huh," said Lenny. "Aw fuck it, they's too sharp for such nonsense. No, I'm thinkin...I'm thinkin our best chance is to jest get the fuck outta here and keep movin. That's my thoughts."

"It is huh?" responded Whitey. "Well fuck, you ain't got the smarts enough ta get us outta here without me and I ain't jest packin up and runnin like I done with the Mesican bandits. Sides, there were more a them than these three. You jest let me do the thinkin, Lenny, yea...jest let me."

Lenny sat mumbling to himself. "Yea you be the thinker Whitey, that's what yer good at all right...thinkin"

Darkness came slowly with the two men not speaking to each other or at all. They kept to themselves the rest of the evening, and by the morning the atmosphere had hardly changed. Lenny and Whitey slowly climbed out of their bedrolls and wandered off in different directions to relieve themselves. Still without speaking, they managed to get the camp packed and ready to go. After quietly making coffee and eating some hardtack and bacon, they packed the remainder of their gear and mounted their horses. Finally the silence was broken when Lenny hocked and spat.

"Damn, Lenny, I didn't think you was ever gonna talk," said Whitey.

Eastern Men

"I ain't," said Lenny. "Least ways not to you anyhow. I guess I ain't got enough smarts ta talk ta you Whitey, so jest leave it be."

Whitey turned his horse southwest and squeezed. Lenny watched for a moment before he took up the lead to the packhorse and followed Whitey down the draw and up onto the plateau. "At least it's a nice fuckin day," he thought.

*****

Sy Common sat back against a rock and exhaled deeply. Never would he have thought the two men he most wanted to see had actually just shown up. He wasn't much a believer in miracles since the mine collapse in Kentucky ten, or so, years ago when his best friend had been crushed under tons of coal. Since then he had been wandering, keeping his head down and not making friends.

The job at the Contention Mine had come at his lowest point and he did his job as best he could. When Dick Gird had accused him of stealing all that gold dust he was crushed. He had never done a dishonest thing in his life. His father, in Virginia, had always told him that 'a man's worth is measured in his steel.' If he were honest and worked hard he would always succeed. Good words from a man that was a god to Common, until the Great Rebellion took his father at an early age. He had been killed in Pennsylvania at a shit hole named Gettysburg and shortly after, his mother had succumbed to fever. Alone at thirteen, Common left Virginia never to return or even look back.

Common looked at the Hunter redressing the poor man that had come running in on the big white mule, now lying dead. He shook his head in almost a smile as he listened to the Hunter lambaste the man.

"Jesus Christ Mr. Bellflower, when I tell you ta stay put, that's what I fuckin mean stay the fuck put! That's my favorite fuckin mule damn you," the Hunter yelled. He walked over to the mule and could see he was dead, shot through the head. Squatting down he patted the mule's head and stood. "This is just fuckin great." He said.

"I had to Hunter," said Phineas feeling somewhat embarrassed.

"Yea, yea why'd ya have to Mr. Bellflower?" asked the Hunter sarcastically.

"Because Whitey Wellford and Lenny Bristol were shooting at me," answered Phineas and he sat heavily on a rock, putting his head in his hands.

"Appears ta me he had reason ta not listen, Mr. Hunter," said Stryker. "Hell, I guess getting a tongue lashin from you is a far better outcome than bein buried because a them two toadies."

"I have ta agree, Mr. Hunter. Seems this fella was jest tryin ta get outta the way a some fast flowin lead himself…much the same as us I guess," said Common.

The Hunter softened a bit. Looking around, his gaze fell on the dead Apache, no more than eighteen or nineteen. "Don't worry about it Mr. Bellflower, we'll work it out somehow," said the Hunter. "Damn fine mule though…damn fine." He walked back to the rock Common was sitting against and leaned against it to ease the weary bones in his body. "Where's yer stock Common?"

Common got up and stretched his arms over his head. "A little canyon right behind you. Funny thing is, them Apaches done any scoutin they coulda took em easy and I woulda never been the wiser." He pulled a piece of jerky from his vest pocket and took a bite, offering it to the other two men, they declined and he shoved it back into his pocket. "I'll go get em and we can figure out what we're gonna do for Mr. Bellflower here." Common set off to the north end of the small ridge.

Stryker watching him leave looked over at the Hunter. "He showed a lot of sand today, Mr. Hunter," said Stryker. "

Eastern Men

"He did at that," said the Hunter.

Ten minutes later Common walked back into the campsite leading his horse, a mule and two ponies left by the Apaches. "Found these two grazin by my stock, thought we could use em," said Common.

The Hunter walked to the ponies. Both were stout and obviously well fed and both were shod. "Ranch horses," he said. "Well, Mr. Bellflower, it appears you have yer own mount now. Pick one."

Phineas stood up and walked to the two horses. "I don't know anything about horses Hunter. This one here looks nice." He pointed to the smaller of the two. A pinto with four white socks and a star blaze on his forehead. Approaching slowly, he patted the horse on the neck and gently stroked his shoulder. "He'll do just fine Hunter, just fine.

"Well, one thing sure, you ain't gonna be sittin on any more packs. It's real good Apaches like saddles other than bareback," said Stryker. "Leaves us another horse for our packs too, Mr. Hunter."

The Hunter looked at Stryker, and then over at Phineas as he stood stroking the horse. "Well, Mr. Bellflower, lets get that animal stripped and we'll get camp set up for the night. We'll be leavin early in the mornin." He looked at Common. "You comin with us Common?"

Common stood and looked at the Hunter thinking. Finally, seeming to make up his mind, he spoke. "Yea, yea, think I will. Don't want ta chance getting caught by them 'paches again…that's for damn sure."

"Hunter, perhaps you should issue me a weapon," said Phineas. "Perhaps if the red Indians return, I will be able to help in the fray." Phineas stared at the rigging of the saddle totally lost as to what to do with it or how to remove it.

The Hunter glanced at Phineas while he unsaddled Bandit. "I don't think so. Mr. Bellflower, don't think there's a need and we're better off leavin the shootin to those that know how."

Stryker went to Phineas' aid. "Here, Mr. Bellflower, let me show you." Deftly Stryker untied the cinches and walked around the other side of the horse and flipped the cinches over the saddle along with the right stirrup fender. Going back to the other side, he lifted the saddle and the blanket from the horse, walked over and dropped it by Common's old campfire. Moving back to the horse, Stryker again spoke to Phineas. "In the mornin, Mr. Bellflower, I'll show you how to saddle and bridle him too."

Eastern Men

"Thank you, Mr. Stryker, kind of you," said Phineas. "And, I suppose I do agree with you about the weapon, Hunter. Between you and Mr. Stryker and Mr. Common, you three seem to have the knack of the fight tied down."

In the waning light of the day, the four men leaned against saddles drinking coffee and talking of their lives. Each man took a turn talking about themselves and major events in their lives. The Hunter was surprised by the lively life Phineas Bellflower had lived. He spoke of the article outlining the criminality of Big Mike McManus and the fifth ward, the two thugs on his trail, Spats and Mr. O'Brien and his quest for the story of the Arizona Territory. The real story, not the exaggerated briefs popping up in some of the nations dailies.

Phineas had, of course, heard of the famous, or infamous, Earp brothers, the cowboys and their dealings. Cochise County where it all happened was his target. He wanted to be where the street fight took place, see the actual locales surrounding Tombstone and Charleston and maybe meet some of the actual participants. But first, first he had to evade Spats and Mr. O'Brien.

Eastern Men

Phineas finally finished his story and lay back on his saddle. "I haven't talked that much in years," he said. "Feels good to get it all out.

"Tell me more about this Spats and O'Brien," said the Hunter. "How dangerous are they really?"

"Well, Hunter, let's say that as enforcers for McManus, they are at the top of their game. They're mean and tough. They both grew up in Hells Kitchen in the city. Learned early about the gun, the knife and the sap. Spats' real name is Michael Melloy and O'Brien is James O'Brien. They're tight, tight as can be. I know they're following me and they won't quit until they catch me or I am dead…the end result being the same I'm afraid." Phineas stopped talking. Thinking hard for a moment. "You won't have any trouble recognizing them, Hunter. They are going to be looking a bit out of place out here."

"Somethin like you?" asked Sy Common.

"Precisely, Mr. Common, precisely," replied Phineas. "Only Spats and Mr. O'Brien will be armed and schooled in the weapons they carry."

Stryker sat up and poured himself more coffee then lay back on his saddle. "I think we're pretty schooled with our weapons too, Mr. Bellflower."

Eastern Men

"You have no idea," the Hunter thought smiling. "No idea at all."

NINE

Lenny stirred the ashes for a spark or the glow of an ember. "Damn Whitey forgot to bank the fuckin fire again last night," he thought. He reached into his coat pocket and rummaged for a match, when he finally located one, he noticed there was no kindling around either. "Fuck, Whitey! Ya coulda got some kindling or at the very fuckin least, banked the fuckin fire," Lenny yelled.

Whitey came out of a sound sleep and looked at Lenny stomping around the camp. "What the fuck are you hollerin at, Lenny?' he asked. "It's too fuckin early ta be stompin around like that, lest it's cold and it ain't that cold."

Lenny stopped and looked at Whitey. "Ya want some coffee, Whitey?" he asked. "Or meybe some breakfast?"

Whitey sat up awake now. "Damn, Lenny, you did all that this mornin? You bet! I'm hungry."

"No, I didn't do that," Lenny said. We don't have coffee, we don't have breakfast, wanna know why, Whitey, really wanna know?" He kicked a rock across the clearing. "Because we ain't got fire, Whitey, WE AIN'T GOT FUCKIN FIRE!" Lenny yelled.

Whitey stared at Lenny like a deer caught in a torch. "I guess I forgot," he said quietly.

Eastern Men

There were things he stopped at with Whitey, but the things he got most worked up over were the things Whitey forgot to do. Like banking the fire. Each one had jobs to do and if one didn't do theirs, it would throw the balance off, not that there was much of a balance with Whitey and Lenny

So, quietly Whitey did what he should. "Lenny, I'm sure sorry about the fire again…seems I been forgettin that little chore lately." He scratched his head.

"Meybe ya jest ain't got the smarts ta think about them fires, Whitey," said Lenny.

"I'll get some kindling…be back in a couple a minutes." Whitey walked off towards the arroyo there he knew he could find some mesquite.

*****

Mr. O'Brien scratched through the ashes looking for a coal, a spark, anything to get the fire going again but finally resigned himself the fact that he was going to have to rebuild it again. "How the hell do they do that out here and keep it going all night?" he asked himself.

"Who you talkin to Jamie?" Spats sat up in his bedroll and stretched. "Ain't no one here but us two."

"Damn fire is out again," Mr. O'Brien said. Sighing heavily, he accepted it that as two eastern men, they were terrible at outdoors things.

Eastern Men

TEN

Jeff Stryker came over the rise and spotted the tracks he had been looking for. Urging Waco forward, he trotted his horse to where the tracks came into plain view. Stepping down he knelt next to one of the tracks. Studying it carefully he noted the lack of a sharpness and crispness in the tracks and he guessed them to be almost two days old. Stryker stood and looked off at the direction of travel. "Two days," he thought. "Two days in front. They could be anywhere by now."

He remounted and turned his horse back to the other three men almost a mile in the rear. As he trotted up the rise he spurred Waco and the horse went into a nice easy ground-chewing lope.

The country where they were now was bothersome. Bothersome in the sense that it had a lot of small hills and arroyos dotting the landscape and Stryker had to be careful where Waco's next step was. Still he loped on, watchful for a hole or edge that could quickly deteriorate and throw horse and rider down into an arroyo or roll them down a hill.

Finally after five or six minutes, Stryker rounded a small rock formation and rode up to the Hunter. "I found their track, Mr. Hunter, but they are still two days from us, near as I can tell."

The Hunter rose and walked to Bandit grazing on some desert grass. Tightening his cinch, he re-bridled Bandit and swung into the saddle. Turning to Phineas, he noticed that Phineas had fallen asleep.

"Mr. Bellflower!" yelled the Hunter. "Wake up and let's get movin." He stood in his stirrups and sat back down adjusting his seat.

Phineas slowly came out of the nap and looked around. "I see Mr. Stryker has returned," he said. "Give me a moment and I will be aboard that horse, a most disagreeable mount, I may add." He rose yawning and moved to his horse where he tightened his cinch and also re-bridled his mount. Climbing up he finally got seated in the saddle. "I swear, Hunter, how you men do this day after day escapes me." He fidgeted for a few moments trying to ease the constant pain in his backside. When finally he decided it was as good as it was going to get he looked to the Hunter. "All right, I am now ready to depart."

Sy Common sat on his horse and watched Phineas a bemused grin on his face. "It ain't hard, Mr. Bellflower...ya jest climb on and try ta stay put is all...the horse does the rest."

"And what, sir, is to account for these blisters I am currently experiencing on my backside?' asked Phineas. "The horse doing the work you say?'"

"No sir," said Common. "That there is jest plain poor horsemanship." He laughed out loud. "Ain't no one gonna attest to your abilities aboard that nag there, Mr. Bellflower. Least ways no one here anyhow."

The Hunter sat listening to the exchange. "Seems to be agreeable to a bit a funning." He thought. "Let's get. Jeff, you lead," he said.

"Yessir, Mr. Hunter." Stryker turned his horse back in the direction he had just come and slowly rode back out to the tracks he had found earlier.

*****

Mr. O'Brien stood next to his horse and took a large drink of water. Pulling out a kerchief, he wiped his head and neck before stuffing the cloth back into his pocket.

"I'm lost," said Mr. O'Brien.

"What did yous say, Jamie?" asked Spats.

"I said I'm lost Mickey…I'm fuckin lost," Mr. O'Brien said. "I'm sure I followed the compass to the letter. Dammit, now we gotta go back a ways and see where we went wrong."

"Where we went wrong," said Spats. "I ain't even seen the fuckin compass since we been out here, Jamie. That would be…well that would be where you went wrong."

"We, me, it doesn't matter, Mickey. The simple fact of it is that we are lost. That's both of us, unless you aren't lost and if that's the case, how about you showin me which way to go," said Mr. O'Brien.

"Not me, I'm a follower," said Spats then he turned and found a rock to sit on. He had just sat when he heard an angry buzzing coming from behind the rock. He jumped up and spun around. Cautiously walking around the rock at a safe distance, he spotted a coiled rattlesnake, his head bobbing and weaving, obviously extremely agitated, his tail buzzing loudly in the early afternoon quiet. "Look at the size a that snake, Jamie…must be five or six feet long. Spats leaned forward to get a better look.

Mr. O'Brien pulled Spats back. "Jesus, Mickey, that snake can jump you know," he said.

Spats reached into his pocket and withdrew his .32 Ivor Johnson revolver. "I can shoot him," he said.

"With that? You'll just piss him off, Mickey" said Mr. O'Brien. He turned and walked to their packhorse and withdrew a short eight gauge double-barreled shotgun from under the manty then returned to where Spats stood poised with his short pistol. "Here, use this."

Spats looked at Mr. O'Brien hold out the shotgun. A smile spread across his face as he took the shotgun from Mr. O'Brien, pointed it at the snake and pulled the trigger. The explosion rocked the desert around them. The snake was lifted and blown against some rocks, finally coming to rest, blown into pieces by the force of the double-ought buckshot. "I hear ya can eat em," said Spats.

"Nah, can't eat em... probably get poisoned or something," admonished Mr. O'Brien.

"Yea, probly," replied Spats.

"Let's stop fooling about. We have to get back on the right track." Mr. O'Brien took the shotgun from Spats and pushed it back under the manty on the packhorse. Grabbing his reins, he mounted his horse, trying to adjust his sore backside to the now immensely uncomfortable saddle.

Spats walked back to his horse and put his foot in the stirrup then stopped. Pulling his foot back out he flipped the stirrup fender over the saddle and tightened his cinch then mounted. Pulling off his hat he scratched his head and repositioned his hat. "No way I'm gonna do that again," he said.

Eastern Men

When both men were mounted they started backtracking themselves hoping to find where they made the mistake. The truth was that the mistake they made was counting on a compass in country that was full of metal ore and high magnetic fields and that just wasn't going to get them anywhere.

Eastern Men

ELEVEN

Whitey Wellford stood in his stirrups and looked out over the country and especially focusing in on the eight or so riders in the distance. It was a pretty safe bet that if he saw them, they probably saw him. He wasn't sure, but he was fairly certain they were Apaches and probably up to no good. He sat back into his saddle and turned his horse. Riding back to where Lenny and the pack mule waited, his thoughts turned to money and spending money in a nice town. In fact he was so deeply into thinking about the money, he almost rode right past Lenny and the mule.

"Hey Whitey, wake up!" Lenny yelled. "We're over here," he motioned.

Whitey started. "Shit, musta been day dreamin for sure." He reined in and turned his horse. "I was thinkin on that money, Lenny. I would sure like ta get somwer and spend some a it pretty damn soon."

Lenny spit and looked at Whitey. "Don't wanna go ta Tombstone, Breakenridge'll jest throw us out agin." He rubbed his jaw a moment. "How bout Contention City? They got some nice saloons there I bet, and they don't know us there neither."

109

Eastern Men

Whitey pointed in the direction he had just come from. "'paches ridin southwest a here, bout eight or so. I'm guessin up ta no good." He dismounted and tightened his cinch. "So, where's it gonna be, Lenny?"

Lenny studied the question for a moment. "Anywhere them 'paches ain't," he replied. "I ain't in no mood ta be fightin and runnin from them fuckin 'paches. Myself, I have much better fuckin things ta be worryin about…like, a cold beer and a woman."

Whitey remounted his horse and turned to Lenny. "What woman is gonna want ta be with the likes a you, Lenny. Hell, ya smell like ya ain't bathed in years and yer clothes are rottin off yer fuckin back." He kicked his horse and started over the rise into the small valley below. He had no idea where they were headed, but he knew it was the opposite direction of the Apaches he had seen, and right now that was just fine with him.

Three hours later they heard the gunfire and caught sight of the gun smoke by a hill in the foothills of the Huachuca Mountains. Riding slowly, they came up on the eight Apaches Whitey had seen earlier and they had two men down fighting for their lives.

Eastern Men

Lenny looked at Whitey, a question on his face. "Well," he said. "We gonna be fuckin Samaritans today or not, cause if we are…I hope we got some medicated papers left cause, I'm gonna shit my fuckin pants" Lenny pulled his big Remington pistol out and pointed it at the scene below.

"Leave the fuckin mule here," said Whitey. "Aw fuck, let's get."

Both men spurred their horses down the hill into the midst of the fight in progress. Lenny's horse got there first and raced in between the bullets fired from the rocks above. Jumping from his horse he pulled his Marlin repeater out of the saddle boot and jumped from his horse feeling his right ankle sprain as he hit the ground forcing him to crab crawl to the two men.

Whitey galloped in and pulled his Winchester and joined the men on the ground.

"How long you boys been hole up here?" asked Lenny in between shots.

"About two hours now. They came at us all of a sudden, firing from those rocks. We aren't exactly prepared for an Apache fight," said Mr. O'Brien.

Whitey looked around and all he could see was a short double barrel and the second fellow holding a small revolver. "Jesus," he thought. "What the hell are these boys doing out here?"

Whitey hocked and spat. "That peashooter workin fer ya?" he asked the fellow with the small revolver.

"Think I need a bigger gun," said Spats.

A rifle ball whined in and thunked at the foot of Spats. He yanked his foot in as far as he could. "You boys give me the loan of a rifle?" he asked.

Lenny handed his Marlin over to Spats. "Ya know how ta work one a them mister?"

"I think I can work it out," said Spats. He raised the rifle to his shoulder and squeezed the trigger but nothing happened. He tried again with no better results.

Frustrated, Lenny grabbed the rifle back and worked the lever shoving a cartridge into the chamber and handing it back to Spats. "They call it a lever gun for a reason, mister." He reached down and pulled off his boot, rubbing his ankle that was quickly swelling. "Fuck, musta broke it…dammit," he mused.

The firing stayed general and started to taper off after about twenty minutes, the Apaches staying around for another twenty or thirty minutes occasionally throwing shots down, then started filtering out until all that was left were the four men in the canyon, one with a badly sprained ankle and a bad disposition.

"A course this had a happen now. Fuckin foot, jest fuckin cut it off and be done with it," Lenny hissed.

Whitey scooted over to Lenny and checked out his sprain. "Ain't broke, Lenny. Tore up a bit, but ain't broke and ya ain't gonna be able ta get that boot on fer awhile I guess," he said. He pinched his nose. "But that foot stinks somethin awful."

"Yea, well fuck you too," said Lenny. Then he looked over at Spats and Mr. O'Brien. "Where you boys comin from or goin. You're sure dressed peculiar ta be galavantin around out here."

Mr. O'Brien exhaled a large breath of air and eyed the two rough looking men in front of him. "Appreciate the assistance gents." Leaning back against a rock he looked up at the rock walls that had held the Apaches. "The stable owner warned us about just this. When it got real quiet, we didn't pay attention and we should have." He leaned forward and stood up. "Are they gone now?" Mr. O'Brien asked.

"Looks ta be," responded Whitey. "Near as I can tell anyhow." He got to his feet and walked over to get his horse. Mounting he turned to the small group. "Riding out ta get the packs, Lenny, you stay put, y'hear?" Turning his horse,

Eastern Men

Whitey trotted back to the little ridge and gathering the packhorse, turned and made his way back down to the men.

Lenny sat and watched, occasionally looking at Spats and Mr. O'Brien, wondering what they were doing so far out in nowhere. And, what they were doing out there in the clothing they were wearing.

Mr. O'Brien eyed Lenny. Never being one to trust another human being other than Spats, he naturally wondered how it was that the two itinerant hands happened upon them at such a fortuitous moment. The only logical conclusion would have to be that Lenny and Whitey had been following them.

Lenny took in the clothing of the two men. The only reason they would be dressed that way in the desert was if they were Pinkertons, Pinkertons sent to trail and trap he and Whitey. That had to be it. They were Pinkertons.

Whitey rode back into the group and dismounted. From the packs he pulled a length of muslin and tore a strip long enough to wrap Lenny's ankle. Turning to walk to Lenny, Whitey stopped and looked at the three men. The one called O'Brien was sitting with his shotgun across his lap haphazardly pointing it in Lenny's direction. The other one called Spats, was leaning against a rock twirling his little pistol around his finger watching Lenny. And Lenny was seated holding his Remington pistol in his lap pointed at O'Brien and watching Spats.

"What the fuck," said Whitey. "I'm gone five minutes and you three can't even be civil."

"Why are you following us," said Mr. O'Brien.

Whitey looked at Mr. O'Brien and then at Lenny. "Is that what this here's about?" he asked. "I'll be dipped in shit. We ain't followin you boys."

"Yea, well they're fuckin Pinkertons, Whitey," said Lenny. "Otherwise why would they be dressed like that? Bowler hats and the fuckin like." Lenny adjusted his seat, laying his pistol aside for the time being. "Now why you fuckin Pinkertons followin us mister, huh?"

"We're not Pinkertons, and we weren't following you," said Mr. O'Brien. "We're looking for someone else" he paused. "So why were you two here so quick if you weren't following us?"

Whitey looked at Mr. O'Brien. "We just happened ta be coming this direction and heard the shootin," he said. "Next time we'll know better and go the opposite way so's we don't have ta listen to the likes a you."

Spats shoved his pistol back into his pocket and sat down. "I'll be dammed," he said. "A fuckin accident."

Eastern Men

Whitey squatted down and started to wrap Lenny's ankle then he stopped and looked at the two eastern men. "Yer lookin fer who exactly?"

"You wouldn't know him. Someone we knew in New York," Said Mr. O'Brien. "We followed him from New York to Chicago then here and he disappears in the desert." Mr. O'Brien looked over at Spats as he worked to put some coffee on the fire he had just built. Turning back to Whitey and Lenny, Mr. O'Brien sighed and sat back. "We have no idea now where he might have gone, which is why we are on our way to Tombstone. He may have gone there, he's a writer."

Whitey and Lenny looked at each other in astonishment. "It can't be Phineas Bellflower," they each thought.

"This feller got a name?" asked Lenny.

"Yes...Phineas Bellflower," answered Mr. O'Brien.

Again the two men looked at each other.

"Never heard a him," said Whitey. "Well, Lenny, we best be gettin, ain't no reason ta be holdin on here no more."

"Awright, help me get on my horse can ya?" Lenny gathered his rifle and boot and hobble to his horse. Sliding the rifle in the rifle boot and shoving his boot in his saddlebags, he waited for Whitey. When Whitey got there, he lent a shoulder and Lenny struggled aboard his horse finally seating himself.

Whitey walked over and mounted his horse and took the lead to the packhorse. He turned to the two men on the ground. "Gents, you be watchin fer them 'paches. They're sneaky fuckers sure. Ya jest be watchin yer asses." He turned back in his saddle. "Lets get, Lenny."

Once away from the two men, Whitey turned to Lenny and heaved a sigh of relief. "Who coulda guessed," he said. "They're huntin Mr. Bellflower and they don't appear ta be friendly types at all."

"Fuckin New York assholes," said Lenny. "Shoulda shot em when I had the chance."

Whitey reined in his horse and turned to Lenny. "Whadya think we was doin?" He turned back and started off again. "We left him hogtied in his underwear…kinda thinking, we was thinking, he was gonna expire."

Spats poured some coffee and sat back. "Jamie, they were some mighty peculiar laddies." He took a sip of his coffee and thought for a moment. "Fuckin desert assholes, they looked to me."

Eastern Men

Mr. O'Brien looked up from a rock he was studying. "Indeed," he said. "More desert weasels if you ask me."

Eastern Men

TWELVE

Traveling in a south, southwest direction, the four riders were in no hurry. The Hunter had learned a long time ago that to try to hurry in the desert only depleted necessary stores they could ill afford to lose. The tracks were plain and easy to follow and the three men rode easy. Earlier, Stryker had gone ranging far ahead, watching for tracks and anything of interest to the group.

Sy Common turned in his saddle. "Mr. Hunter, when do ya think we'll be catchin up with those two?"

The Hunter, who had been silent for the better part of an hour, started at the sudden voice. "Jesus, that unnerved me a bit," he said.

"Didn't mean ta startle ya, Mr. Hunter, just askin is all." Common spit a wad of tobacco juice to the ground.

"Thinkin about Jolly I guess," said the Hunter. "I miss 'em somethin terrible sometimes, even though he was one a the worlds largest pains in the ass." The Hunter smiled at that thought. But he did miss his companionship and his insight into people. Jolly could, oft times, read people when the Hunter couldn't get a handle. He had had the gift of sifting through everything and getting to the answer soon enough. Now, with Jolly gone, it was Jeff Stryker that was becoming the comrade in arms. Stryker was also showing the foresight and intuition about people and the Hunter appreciated that gift in both men. After all, Stryker had been right about Sy Common. He had also been right about the Ghost.

Now with Phineas Bellflower taking the trip with them, the hunt for Whitey and Lenny was taking on a different hue. If it hadn't been so dangerous with the Apaches, the Hunter would have thought the entire trip a comedy of errors with Mr. Bellflower in the lead role. "He sure as hell has no business being out here," the Hunter thought to himself. "No business at all."

The Hunter looked up at Common. "Should be a couple more days now. By then we should be in Tombstone, or damn close to it."

"Seems kinda funny goin back that direction," said Common. "What with Dick Gird and all."

"Gird is a bit hot headed, but he's a decent enough man," said the Hunter. "I bet, if you was to ask him, he would probly have a job for you, no questions."

Common reined in his horse and waited for the Hunter to pull up alongside of him. "Are you joking, Mr. Hunter?" asked Common. "Cause if y'are, I'll laugh…if not, it ain't very funny."

Eastern Men

"I ain't jokin, Common. You're a good man and seems to me a practical and cool-headed man. Anyone would be honored to have you as an employee…even Dick Gird. So maybe, just maybe you can be a bigger man and forgive the mistake," said the Hunter. "If ya can't then I understand, but my friend Jolly Goodman used to say; 'If ya'll kin go through life never makin a fuckin mistake, then don't bother to go fuckin swimmin, you'll just be walkin on the fuckin water.' Kinda says it all I think."

Common looked at the Hunter and then turned forward. "I'll think on it," he said and rode off.

"Jolly, yer one hell of a man," said the Hunter to himself. He turned back to watch Phineas adjust again in his saddle. "Mr. Bellflower, ya just have ta get used to it. The more ya fidget, the more ya hurt, and don't be bouncing around on that horse, you'll hurt his back."

"Well, Hunter, the mere truth of the matter is that my behind has been raw for the last few days, so no amount of fidget, or non fidget is going to help at this juncture." Phineas, scooted forward in the saddle thinking, "There is no way I am ever going to heal from this excursion. No way at all."

The Hunter turned his attention forward and caught sight of Jeff Stryker galloping fast towards them. When finally he reined Waco in, the Hunter noticed Stryker to be breathing hard and worry was set on his face.

"Mr. Hunter, we gonna have company pretty soon I guess," he said. "Them damn Apaches are gatherin up ahead about two-three miles and they don't look ta be real friendly and, it appears they added some ta their number." Stryker dismounted and stood leaning against his horse. Taking a drink from his canteen, he hung it back on his saddle and turned towards the Hunter. "They already seen us, Mr. Hunter, ain't a lot we kin do now but wait or hit first."

The Hunter cupped his hands over his mouth and called back to Common and Phineas. When they joined he and Stryker, the Hunter dismounted and taking a drink from his canteen, he cleared his throat and spoke. "Appears as we ain't shuck a those Apaches just yet. Stryker says they're in front a us a couple miles." He cleared his throat, hocked and spat. Thinking for a moment he resumed. "Seems to me and Jeff here we got a couple choices. We can move forward and hope they're just sniffin around, we can stay here and see what happens, or we can set up our own surprise."

"What do you mean, Hunter? What sort of surprise can we set up, as you say?" Phineas asked, finally climbing from his horse. "After all, there are a mere four of us against mounted, well armed hostiles."

Eastern Men

"The truth of it, Mr. Bellflower is there's only three fightin men here. No offense, but I don't want to hand you a gun and have you shoot me," said the Hunter. "Least ways not right now anyhow."

"I say we give em a taste," said Common. "I wasn't too happy scrunched behind them rocks a ways back, I expect they won't be neither." Common dismounted and checked his cinch, making sure everything was secure on his saddle. "Any place ta give em a jolt, Jeff?"

Stryker thought for a moment then turned back towards the way he had come. "Yea, I guess there is. See that gap out there where them rocks go all jagged at the top?"

The other three men looked out over the vista and found the spot Stryker was talking about

"Well, seems ta me, them 'paches gotta come right through that gap, they wanna get ta us or they wanna catch us there…if we beat em there, we can be waitin when they come ridin up." He pulled his hat and scratched his head. "We ain't gonna get em all, but we can get some. Them 'paches don't like surprises and we give one good enough, well, I think they'll light out agin." He put his hat back on. "We better be moving or we could be ridin right inta them."

The Hunter pushed his hat back and rubbed his neck. Since his haircut, his neck was constantly sunburned and silently, he made a vow to let his hair grow and never cut it again. Looking around at the group he pulled his hat back down. "If we're goin, let's get," he said and mounted Bandit. "How long ya think we have, Jeff?"

"I'm guessin 'bout twenty minutes maybe less," answered Stryker as he too mounted his horse.

The Hunter looked over at Phineas. "Unless you expect that horse to ride you, I would be getting mounted. We are gonna have to make a dash of it as it is."

Phineas sighed heavily and remounted his horse, turning it towards the gap they would be making for. "I guess I'm ready, Hunter."

"I guess you better be, Mr. Bellflower." With that he spurred Bandit and took off for the gap in the wall of mountains in front of them.

Racing across the valley floor, the four men concentrated on getting to the pass before the Apaches could, or realize that was what their quarry was going to do.

For a full five minutes the four men galloped their horses before finally arriving at the gap. The Hunter and Stryker dismounted, pulling their Winchesters and handing the reins to Phineas.

Eastern Men

"Take the horses behind those rocks over there," the Hunter pointed at a group of large rocks. "Stay there, and for Christ's sake, stay down this time."

Common handed his reins to Phineas as well and all three men climbed the jagged rocks looking for good shooting positions.

Shielding his eyes from the fierce sun, Stryker poked his head around some rocks and saw the Apaches still almost a half mile distant but coming at a trot. Quickly counting, he counted twenty-seven warriors all well mounted and appearing to be well armed.

Tossing a small rock at the Hunter, he flashed his hands to tell the Hunter the count of Apaches then settled down in his position with his Winchester at the ready.

The Hunter nodded, turned to Common and gave him the same count and got ready and he didn't have long to wait.

A few minutes later the Apaches rode into their killing field and halted. Dismounting, the Apache in the lead squatted and looked at Stryker's earlier tracks then looked out in the distance. Standing up, he walked to the group and hurriedly said something, then vaulted back onto his horse.

The crash of the three rifles was almost in unison as the three men in the rocks poured rifle fire into the group of surprised and confused Apaches. Immediately three Apaches reeled and dropped from their horses and tried to crawl away, but caught another rifle ball for their efforts. With out a break the three men poured fire into the retreating Apaches but one by one they would turn and try to make an assault on the rocks being forced back every time.

When the firing slackened then stopped, the Hunter motioned to Stryker to go back to the packs and get more ammunition, then he leaned back and reloaded his Winchester. When he looked over at Common, he saw him doing the same with a wide grin across his face.

The Hunter shook his head and put his attention back onto the group of Apaches milling about in the distance. Taking a quick count, he counted the bodies in front of them and came up two short. Again he counted the group and the bodies and again came up short.

"Shit!" yelled the Hunter. "Two of em are tryin ta get in behind us," he yelled as Stryker came up with the Ammunition. "Jeff" he yelled. "Me and Common can handle things here…you get over ta them rocks over there and watch for them other two."

Stryker signaled okay, immediately tossing the ammunition to the Hunter and started the climb back over to the rocks directly above where Phineas waited with the animals.

Shoving cartridges into his Winchester, he surveyed the craggy surface of the ridge until he could spot an area likely to be the path of the two Apaches. Moments later he heard the firing begin again in earnest and his eyes sharpened, watching the ridgeline.

In one minute, he was rewarded with the sight of an Apache slowly coming into view as he struggled across the rocks, making his way to the horses and Phineas. Stryker waited until the other Apache was in sight before he raised his rifle to fire. Drawing aim on the second Apache, he took a deep breath, started exhaling and squeezed. His rifle bucked into his shoulder and the Apache's head snapped forward, then backwards as he dropped like a stone. Quickly swinging his rifle downward, he took aim at the first Apache and fired. The ball hit the Apache just under his left breast and the shock reeled him backwards onto a rock then bounced him onto a fairly flat stone and he lay there unmoving.

The fire continued in the canyon and Stryker moved back over the rocks to his original position, again taking up the fight and driving the remaining Apaches back a second time.

Eastern Men

When quiet prevailed, the Hunter pushed his hat back and exhaled. "I don't think they will want to try it again, but these are Apache, and never know what they're gonna do." He pulled his bandana from his neck and wiped his face and neck. "One thing sure," said the Hunter. "They know where we are and how many we are. They ain't against fightin at night neither, so they may be comin back in tonight."

Common stood up and stretched. "That felt right nice," he said again grinning.

"Ain't nuthin to grin about Common. Killin ain't supposed to be fun, it's just killin is all and not a particularly pleasant occupation." The Hunter stood and taking up his Winchester, he turned to Common. "You stay here on watch, Jeff and me are gonna go get some coffee started and somethin to eat." The Hunter turned back to Stryker and together, the two men descended to Phineas and their packs.

Phineas Bellflower lay in his blankets shivering. The night had gotten cold, but he suspected it was the remnants of the day making him shiver. The firing from the ridge today had scared him more than he could ever remember. The thought of being overpowered and caught by the marauding Apaches filled him with such a dread, he couldn't even fathom the idea.

Eastern Men

The memory of looking up and seeing Stryker calmly shoot the two Apaches descending on him made him wonder about the strengths of these frontier men. The way in which Stryker had dispatched the two Apaches then calmly returned to the fight, left him in awe of their temerity and dedication to each other.

Phineas rolled onto his side and looked at the two sleeping forms rolled in blankets. Quietly he rose, and pulling his coat around his shoulders he went to relieve himself then scaled the ridge to a form sitting silently in the darkness watching and listening.

"Mr. Bellflower, you should be getting some rest, tomorrow is comin early," said Stryker as he turned to see Phineas approaching in the dark.

"How did you know it was me Jeff?" asked Phineas. "I thought I was being quite silent."

"Well, sir, there's just somethin about the way a man moves that ain't from here, specially when he ain't used ta climbin around in the dark." Stryker picked up his coffee cup and took a drink, setting the cup back down beside him. "Sides, yer wearing them thin soled city shoes and they make a funny noise on the rocks...kinda like a squeak."

Eastern Men

Phineas sat on a rock and looked at Stryker. "Mr. Stryker, you amaze me. Is there anything that gets by you, ever?" Phineas asked.

"Sure, lotsa things, Mr. Bellflower, but when I'm sittin here in the middle of the night watchin for Apaches, you gotta know I'm gonna hear a toad fart at a hunnert yards," said Stryker.

Phineas clapped his hand on his knee. "Bravo, Mr. Stryker. Now that was first hand stuff!"

Stryker put his finger to his lips. "Shhhhh, Mr. Bellflower. If them Apaches are still around, they'll hear ya and start throwing rifle balls up here."

"Of course, sorry Mr. Stryker...I'll just be leaving you then," said Phineas. He slowly stood upright and started making his way back to the camp and the small amount of safety he felt there.

Eastern Men

THIRTEEN

Mr. O'Brien was struggling with tightening the cinch on his horse. "Dammit, I can't seem to get the hang of this contraption." He stepped back and surveyed the gear again, hoping that it would magically tie itself. "I am getting pretty tired of this blasted desert and all the infernal little creatures bandying about." He stepped back to the horse and began anew to try to tie the cinch.

Since trying to get to Tombstone, they had been attacked by Apaches, run into two itinerant morons, been bitten, stung and scared half witless and now, the cinch was causing problems.

Mr. O'Brien walked away from the horse in disgust. He sat on a rock and picked up his coffee cup and started to take a drink when he saw the small spider that had crawled in and was floating on his coffee. He immediately flung the cup across the camp and got up stomping. Not a man to use profanity, he let loose a string of expletives that would have made Jolly Goodman blush.

"God dammit, son of a bitch, this fucking desert has fucking got me pissed off now! I ever get my hands on that Mike fucking McManus or fucking Phineas fucking Bellflower, I swear to you, Spats…well, if I get a hold of them anyway." The anger now spent, he retrieved his cup and put more coffee in it and sat back down.

Spats sat and watched his friend. Only twice had he seen Mr. O'Brien that angry, and the time before he had made the mistake of trying to calm him down. His repayment had been a broken nose and two cracked ribs. No, he knew better than to get within striking range when Mr. O'Brien was angry like that. It was always a prudent gesture to wait it out because it never lasted long. When he finally saw Mr. O'Brien seated again, he spoke.

"Take it easy, Jamie. I'll help ya with the gear. We got bigger problems now though." Spats pointed to the sky. "We got rain comin."

Mr. O'Brien looked skyward just when the first of the fat, heavy raindrops began falling from the heavens. Within a matter of seconds, it was raining so heavily that it was hard to see farther than fifteen feet in front of them.

Spats and Mr. O'Brien raced to get their gear under the canvas manty. Spats ran to the horses and unsaddled them throwing saddle blankets over the gear there. Pulling his coat over his head, he made it back to the main camp where Mr. O'Brien was struggling with the canvas sheet. The wind had picked up and he was trying to get rocks on the corners to hold it in place, quite unsuccessfully. Spats grabbed up some large rocks and put them on the manty to help hold the canvas down. Finally thinking they were done, they stepped back into some rocks that afforded some cover from the pouring rain.

Soaking wet and shivering, the two men stayed put for over an hour as the rain relentlessly pounded from the sky. Occasionally glancing at each other, Mr. O'Brien silently counted the rain in with his list of things he hated about the Arizona Territory.

During the latter part of the second hour they first heard it; the deep rumble of a heavy storm and the cracking of thunder, then something else. A sound that got louder with each minute. A loud swooshing sound that seemed to grow in volume and intensity until it became a roar. Looking to the east, Spats saw it first. A wall of water was rushing at them, affording them little time to save anything but themselves. As quickly as they could they scaled the wet, slippery rocks and when Mr. O'Brien was almost at the pinnacle, the water hit with such intensity, it hurt their eardrums as it rushed past. Just as Spats turned and looked down into the water, he saw saddles and saddle blankets flash by closely followed by three horses, screaming and swimming in the torrential flood.

Eastern Men

Spats elbowed Mr. O'Brien and pointed out the horses sailing by. Mr. O'Brien saw the horses being carried away by the rushing water and dropped his head to his chest sighing mightily. Mentally, he added flash floods to his list.

*****

The Hunter saw the storm approaching and reined in. Scanning the sky, he saw no break in the heavy black clouds and turned to Stryker. "Jeff, we gotta get to high ground now!" He turned to Phineas. "Mr. Bellflower, that's a big storm comin and will surely cause a flash flood. We have to get to high ground as soon as we can."

Spinning Bandit around, he called out to Sy Common. "Common, we gotta get high. You ready?"

"Yessir Mr. Hunter," said Common.

The four men headed, at a run, to a small mesa almost a full two miles away. They had to make it, as dry as it had been, a flood was surely going to try to claim them and their gear.

They loped their horses for ten minutes then trotted for another ten alternating the pace until they reached the mesa. Stryker peeled off and went in search of a way up. Fortunately for them, there was a game trail leading to the top and they began the climb as the first drops started. Quickly, the rain became heavy and it was becoming harder to see the trail yet they continued upward until all four had made the top.

Methodically, they unsaddled and unpacked, staking the horses on short picket lines. As the wind began, the horses and mule turned their hind ends into the wind and stood with their heads down absorbing the brunt of the wind.

The four covered what they could with their canvas and the rest with some slickers sitting on them in the cold rain.

For hours the rain pelted them. There was no sense in trying to talk; the thunder and the roar of the rain would have drowned them out. Then they heard the roar, as the leading edge of the flash flood came into view, taking everything moveable with it.

Phineas sat and watched in awe as the water roared by in with a thunder so loud it caused him to cover his ears.

When finally it began abating, and the sound was not so deafening, Phineas rose and walked to the edge of the mesa looking into the slowing swirling, filthy water as it flowed past.

"I have never, ever in my life, experienced anything like that," Phineas said, when he could talk without yelling. He walked back to their packs, pulling his coat off and laying it on a rock. "I have also never been so wet in my life," he said. He stood; stripping his clothing, hoping it would dry soon enough.

The Hunter surveyed the gear, hoping the dry goods stayed dry and he was rewarded with dry flower, cornmeal and various items. "Putting the slickers over the dry goods was a good idea, Jeff, kept all our food dry."

"Good," answered Stryker. He walked to the horses and uncovered their gear. Although the blankets were sopped, they had done a remarkable job of keeping the gear fairly dry. He reached into his saddlebags and pulled his curry brush out. Going to Waco, he started brushing out his coat helping him dry faster and before long all of the men were doing the same thing.

The Hunter scanned the sky. "Looks to be over," he said. "Least ways for now. We better stay here tonight, give that trail a chance to dry out a bit. I would hate to be the first one over the edge today." He finished brushing out Bandit and returned to the supplies, gathering what wood was available for a fire, which wasn't much after the storm, but it would have to do for tonight.

Struggling with what dry tinder he could find, the Hunter finally got a fire going. It was a smoky, messy fire, but it was fire and they could eat hot food and coffee for the night.

Eastern Men

While the Hunter started getting coffee on and food prepared, Common, Stryker and Phineas bedded the horses down for the night, graining and watering them. Tonight they got extra grain, payment for a good days work and because the fodder was scarce.

When the men were all settled, the Hunter pulled a bottle of Old Tub from his saddlebags and passed it to Sy Common. Common took a drink and passed it to Phineas who also took a drink passing it to Stryker. When it got to Stryker, he simply passed it back to the Hunter who also took a drink and corked the bottle.

"Don't drink Jeff?" asked Common. "Hell a little pull ain't gonna harm ya none."

"No sir, I promised my ma years ago I would never start on the jug. Beer is good enough for me, when I drink that." Stryker settled back into his blankets and yawned. "But y'all go ahead, ain't gonna bother me none."

Common looked at Stryker and sat back. Mind if I have another pull off a that bottle, Mr. Hunter?"

The Hunter passed the bottle back to Common, who in turn started the passing all over again, only this time when the bottle arrived at Jeff Stryker, he was fast asleep and Phineas passed it over the sleeping figure to the Hunter.

"Doesn't take him long does it?" asked Phineas.

Eastern Men

The Hunter took a drink from the bottle, corked it and put it back into his saddlebags. "Mr. Bellflower, let me tell you one thing about Jeff Stryker," he leaned back against his saddle. "You worked as hard as Jeff Stryker does every day, it wouldn't take you long to go to sleep neither." He pulled his hat off and set it aside. Running his hands through his hair and rubbing his neck, he continued. "That boy will be up before any of us in the morning, have the stock taken care of and probably breakfast started."

"I wasn't making an ill comment, Hunter, simply voicing an observation," said Phineas.

"And I was just explaining to you why Jeff is so tired and sleeps the way he does," said the Hunter. "He's one of a million. He and his pard, Bobby Malloy went through a lot before Bobby was killed last year. Jeff took that pretty hard." The Hunter settled into his blankets and let out a big sigh. "I guess we all have been through things to make us better, or worse men, Mr. Bellflower. All of us." He pulled his blanket over him and said, "Now, I am gonna get some sleep and I suggest you both do the same."

Jeff Stryker was finishing packing the panniers when the Hunter walked over to him. "Mr. Hunter, there's somethin about Mr. Bellflower that don't ring right ta me."

Eastern Men

He scratched the dirt with his boot looking for his words. "It's like he's runnin from somethin or someone. He's a writer, sure, but there's more, I think, a lot more than he's sayin now." He looked into the Hunter's face. "Just a feelin, probly don't mean nuthin I guess." Stryker turned and finished the packs.

Watching Stryker work, the Hunter thought over what Stryker had said. He was right. Phineas Bellflower was holding a secret and he just hoped it wasn't a secret that would put all of them in jeopardy. "Damn," he thought. "What did we get into?"

Eastern Men

FOURTEEN

Whitey Wellford, frantically went through the gear they could find. "Dammit," he thought. "Those saddlebags have ta be here somewhere." He continued to rummage through the debris that was once their gear and provisions.

Lenny Bristol climbed to the top of a small hill. Shielding his eyes from the fierce sunlight, he scanned for more of their gear. Finally, he was rewarded with a clump of brown about one hundred yards away. Moving in that direction he broke into a run and in minutes, he was staring at what had been his saddle, and saddlebags that had been filled with money, now just holding a little water in the bottom.

Lenny sat back and stared at the mess in front of him. "Shit!" he yelled out loud and put his head in his hands.

Whitey heard the yell and made his way to where Lenny sat. "Whatcha yellin at, Lenny?" Then he saw the saddle and saddlebags lying in a heap against the little bank. "Shit!" he yelled. "All of it gone?" he asked.

"Lenny looked up. "Yea, every fuckin dollar." Lenny shook his head. "Seems ta me, Whitey, every fuckin time we get somethin, we wind up losin it afore we even have half a fuckin chance to do much with it." Lenny sighed mightily and got up. Picking up the soaked remains of his saddle, he turned back towards where their camp had been.

Whitey stood watching him walk away. "It's too bad," he said. "But he's fuckin right."

For the next two hours, Lenny and Whitey gathered what they could and salvaged what was salvageable from the flood. They had been caught unawares and were barely able to get their animals and themselves to high ground when the water came in with a roar, taking everything else with it. The roar of the water coupled with the pouring rain caused their horses to stomp and snort in fear. It took everything they had to keep their horses calm and keep them from bolting back into the rushing water.

Whitey's saddle had gone only twenty yards before snagging on a bush, mercifully holding until the waters stopped and began to recede. The sawbucks went a bit farther before being launched onto some rocks where they found it later. The panniers were thrown clear but all the stores had been ejected and were soaked clear through including their coats.

In all, the only items salvageable were some blankets, their tack, the sawbucks, panniers and some soggy bacon and beans in the bottom of one of the panniers. All their extra ammunition was scattered around, some washing clean away in the swirling rushing water.

Lenny went in search of some tinder and wood so Whitey could get the fire going. They were in desperate need of dry clothing and in the morning light, Whitey made sure the fire from the wet night out was still banked and would provide a coal for the fire this morning.

When Lenny returned dragging half a mesquite bush and a fat hare he had managed to hit on the head, he saw Whitey sitting back on his heels blowing into a small bundle he held in his hands and the smoke was just starting to rise.

"I brung ya a tree and a surprise," said Lenny as he dragged the mesquite to the fire. "Found this here hare hiding by this bush, so's I grabbed a stick and walloped him a good one and now, we have fresh rabbit for breakfast."

Whitey laid the bundle on top of some small sticks and leaned forward blowing into the wispy smoke until he had a small flame, slowly feeding the fire until they could both hear the crackle and pop of the flames as the wood dried and caught flame.

"I ain't cleanin it," said Whitey, leaning over blowing again on the small flame.

"I ain't cleanin it," Lenny parodied Whitey's comment. "I don't recall askin ya to, asshole." Lenny walked to a rock, knelt down and started dressing out the hare. It took him less than ten minutes to skin and pull the entrails from the rabbit finally piercing it with a stick, he handed it to Whitey, that by now had a nice blaze going.

"What did ya hit it with, Lenny, looks pretty fucked up?" asked Whitey as he leaned the stick holding the rabbit over the fire.

Lenny looked over at Whitey, his face a mask of scorn. "I tolt ya, a fuckin stick…I don't know, meybe it coulda been a club, what the fuck does it matter anyhow, yer gonna eat some fresh rabbit."

"Yum, rabbit," said Whitey. "If this fuckin fire stays lit that is." He looked over at Lenny. "Really, thanks for the rabbit, Lenny," he said and continued to fuss with the fire.

*****

Spats made his way back to where he had left Mr. O'Brien sitting on a mound of dirt in what sparse shade was available from the cactus rising into the air. Picking up a stick, he started tracing out where they were and what was surrounding them.

"Now, Jamie, there are mountains to the south. If you turn yous head, there are mountains to the east and the west too. Only place there ain't no mountains is to the north and that's because," he paused, "That's because there's really big fuckin mountains to the north.

Mr. O'Brien stared at Spats. Unbelieving, he took in what Spats was saying and found himself becoming more and more disturbed.

Spats watched Mr. O'Brien's face carefully, hoping the rage he knew could erupt, wouldn't. "It ain't that bad, Jamie. We coulda been swept away in the flood. Instead we're here and alive."

Mr. O'Brien mumbled something quietly.

"What's that, Jamie?" asked Spats. "What's that you say?"

"I said, for how much longer?" he yelled. "Jesus, I need to be out of this infernal territory." Mr. O'Brien's shoulders slumped and he sat quietly in the narrow shaft of shade.

If ever Spats had seen defeat in his friend, it was right then.

"We don't belong here, Mickey," said Mr. O'Brien quietly. "Mike McManus or Phineas Bellflower be dammed, we have no business being out here at all." He slapped his hands on his knees and rose slowly. "I suppose we better get moving and try to find some water."

Eastern Men

Turning southward, the two men again started off towards the general vicinity of Tombstone and, they hoped, water.

By late afternoon, the sun had been relentlessly beating on them when Mr. O'Brien finally all but collapsed in the long shadow of a boulder and leaned up against it for support. Pulling his sweat stained kerchief from his pocket, he pulled his hat from his head and mopped the sweat streaming into his eyes. Finally putting his bowler back on, he looked over at Spats, doing the very same thing.

Looking over the vista that showed them nothing but more desert and mountains, Mr. O'Brien breathed a loud sigh. "We're never getting out of here, Mickey. I can see the headlines now, in whatever podunk paper is out this way. "Two carcasses, of what can only be assumed were once men, were found in the desert today by a prospector…" Yea, I can see that real clearly."

"Jamie…Jamie!" yelled Spats. "Look there!" He pointed towards the horizon, which, they assumed was northeast.

Approaching them was a dust cloud and tiny specks on the horizon. Silently the two men watched the cloud approach, getting; more and more excited as they finally caught a glimpse of a colorful swallowtail flag flapping in the breeze. That could only mean that they were going to be found by the United States Cavalry.

The column approached slowly until the riders could plainly be seen. The one in the lead appeared to be a civilian and slightly hunched in his saddle. When he caught sight of the two men frantically waving their arms, he broke away and rode directly to them.

Stopping his horse and staring down at the men, a slight smile spread across his face. "You two are about the sorriest lot I seen for a good long while," he said. "Get caught in that squall a while back?"

Mr. O'Brien stepped forward. "A flood sir and it took everything, our horses, our stores, even our weapons, what few we had."

Al Seiber sat on his horse staring at the two men in front of him. "How in the world," he thought. "How in the world have these two managed to survive and keep their skin too?" he asked himself. "You two are damn lucky to get this far with nuthin but yer duds." He dismounted and tightened his cinch. Remounting, he turned back to the two men. "You boys are lucky to be breathin too, there's a passel a real mean Apaches loose and raidin 'round these parts."

Eastern Men

Mr. O'Brien took in the man on the horse. "We have already met some of them. If it hadn't of been for Mr. Wellford and Mr. Bris…"

"Whitey Wellford and Lenny Bristol," said Seiber. "Don't know 'em personal, but I hear they are two a the most worthless men in the territory." Seiber adjusted in his saddle. "Take anything from you?" he asked.

"Not a thing," responded Mr. O'Brien.

"You sure?" asked Seiber. "Them two would take from their mothers, they got half a chance." He looked at Spats. "Your friend there got a tongue?" Seiber looked down at Spat's feet. "And, what's them things on his feet?"

"I got a fuckin tongue and them things on my feet are called spats." Spats moved forward. "Who are yous mister to be talkin to me like that?" Spats puffed out his chest.

"Name's Seiber. Al Seiber, and you two would be…?" asked Seiber.

"I'm Spats Melloy and this gentleman to my left is Mr. O'Brien," said Spats.

"Mr. O'Brien huh," said Seiber spiting into the dirt. "Well, Mr. O'Brien, got a first name?"

"Mister," replied Mr. O'Brien.

Seiber turned in his saddle and waved forward another civilian. When the rider arrived, Seiber gave him quick instructions. "Tom, go back to that Lieutenant there and tell him we got ourselves a couple a sorry cases gonna be travelin with us for a piece."

The rider spun his horse and loped back to the column. The three men watched the Lieutenant bark some orders and then the rider returned with two saddled mounts.

"Lieutenant says these'll have ta do, Al," said the rider.

"Thanks Tom." Seiber turned his horse to the two men. "Them saddles can be a might tricky ta get into. Make sure you grab the horse's mane when getting aboard, it'll help ya," he said. "This here is Tom Horn, gents. Tom, the one with the things on his feet is Spats and the other one is Mr. O'Brien."

"Gents," nodded Horn. "I'll be getting back, Al." Horn turned his horse and again loped back to the column.

"Good boy, but he's got a big mouth and a taste for spirits. Too big a taste y'ask me," said Seiber.

When the two men were mounted, Seiber led them back to the column and before long, they had drunk their fill of water and fell into the rear of the column, riding silently behind and breathing every speck of dust the long column could throw into the air.

Eastern Men

FIFTEEN

Jeff Stryker rode in ever increasing circles looking for the telltale marks of the horses he knew were about somewhere. Ever since coming across the soggy gear, stores and equipment half days ride back; they had all been vigilant for the sight of Whitey and Lenny. They knew it had to be them, at this point they knew nothing about Spats and Mr. O'Brien.

Stryker kept his eyes on the ground looking for the print of a pony that had an inward turn to his right rear leg. For over an hour he scoured the desert and finally, when stopping for a drink of water he happened to look across a cholla break and saw what appeared to be tracks. Quickly hanging his canteen back on his saddle he skirted the cholla and for the first time in hours he was looking at the tracks he wanted.

Stryker thought hard about his next move. With the Hunter, Mr. Bellflower and Sy Common, at least, three hours behind him, it fell on him to track the two bandits.

Stryker dismounted and took his knife from his belt. Finding a suitable donor, he cut three large pieces of mesquite and stripped the thorns and branches. Laying them in an arrow, he marked the trail he would be taking. The

Hunter would be tracking him and would see the circles, and would come across the arrow in the sand. Mounting, he turned Waco to the southwest and squeezed. The horse responded and began following the two sets of tracks Stryker now followed.

"See, Mr. Bellflower, if ya think of the desert as your enemy it will kill ya every time," said the Hunter. "I been ridin this desert here for over thirty-five years and it's true, had my share of mishaps out here, it wasn't ever the desert did it, it was men." The Hunter shifted in his saddle and turned to look at Phineas.

"Hunter, I believe there is something I should inform you about before you and Mr. Stryker find out." Phineas turned in his saddle and looked directly at the Hunter. "There are two thugs from Brooklyn, New York, following me, they have been for over two months now and haven't shown any signs of slacking off." Phineas looked at the Hunter almost pleading with his eyes. "I thought coming to the Arizona Territory would put them off, but I am getting feelings that I think it hasn't."

The Hunter stared at Phineas. "Two thugs huh?" he dismounted and tightened his cinch. Looking up at Phineas, he cleared his throat and spat. "These two thugs, Mr.

Eastern Men

Bellflower, why are they looking for you?" The Hunter looked around. "Good a place as any to noon gents.

Pouring some coffee into his cup, the Hunter leaned back against his saddle and stared at Phineas as the story rolled from his mouth. "They're no different back east," he thought as he listened. When Phineas was done, the Hunter sat up. "So this Mike McManus sent these two, what do you call them, thugs? Mr. Bellflower, it appears, if they are in Arizona, they will most definitely be looking in the larger towns and burgs and we are headed to one of the biggest now, Tombstone." He leaned forward and poured a little more coffee. "This Spats and Mr. O'Brien sound like tough men, Mr. Bellflower, real tough men. But we got somethin they ain't got, and that's the Sonora Desert." The Hunter pushed his hat back on his head, pulled his bandana from his neck and wiped his brow. "This desert will humble any eastern man, Mr. Bellflower."

Re-saddling mounts and preparing to leave, Phineas approached the Hunter. "Hunter, thanks for listening, I was really worried you were going to be furious with me for withholding that information."

"I ain't mad, Mr. Bellflower. I am a might concerned that we have ta start watchin our backs for some other scoundrels other than those two morons, Whitey and Lenny. Just puts us at a bigger risk for getting hurt is all." He finished with saddling Bandit. "Better get mounted, Mr. Bellflower," the Hunter looked over at Common. "You too Common we got ground to make up."

"Jesus, Mr. Hunter, ya think you could call me Sy or Syrus…just plain Common sounds, I don't know, common I guess." Common smiled at his joke.

"Syrus it is," said the Hunter. "Now, Syrus, would you mind getting aboard that horse?" The Hunter mounted his horse. "Syrus, you stay back with Mr. Bellflower. Keep that Colt and Winchester handy, we ain't away from them Apaches yet."

The Hunter turned Bandit and trotted off following Stryker's tracks in the early afternoon.

*****

"I'm hungry," groused Lenny. "We ain't et since yestiddy."

Whitey slid from his horse and started checking him for stones in the shoes. Looking up at Lenny, he replied. "Ain't likely ta til tomorrow neither, so's you'll be a lot more better off ta think about somethin else." Pulling a piece of bush from his horse's tail, Whitey stood straight and looked back over at Lenny. "If'n it makes ya feel any better, I'm damn hungry myself." He turned back to his horse and pulled the saddle and blanket from his back, giving it an opportunity to air out and dry a little before continuing.

Lenny watched Whitey work, finally stepping from his mount and following suit on getting his horse stripped. "Yea, well, we better be getting somethin soon or my belly is gonna be kissin my backbone."

Whitey sat in exasperation. "Jesus, that all you gonna do is bellyache?" he asked.

"Ain't bellyachin, just talkin is all," said Lenny. "Sides, you ain't the one that's gonna say."

Whitey looked at Lenny for a long time before finally speaking. "Say what?"

"When we eat, when we sleep, when we piss…hell, Whitey, I'm getting fuckin tired a you always bein the boss." Lenny stood and walked to some rocks and relieved himself. While walking back he re-buttoned his fly after hitching up his gun belt. When he got back to Whitey, he stood defiantly in front of him. "Gee, I'm sorry, Whitey, I didn't get yer fuckin permission ta piss."

"Yer fuckin making me crazy, Lenny, you really are." Whitey turned and walked away from his friend.

Eastern Men

SIXTEEN

Jeff Stryker made his way through the little canyon hoping there was shade on the other side. The sun had been beating down on him steadily all morning and afternoon and he was ready to give himself a break. The Hunter, Sy and Mr. Bellflower should be about an hour or so behind him if they have been moving at the same pace as he had.

Finally getting through the canyon, he pulled Waco into the shade of the canyon wall and dismounted. Pulling his canteen from his saddle he poured some of the water into his hat and gave it to his horse. Waco eagerly lapped the water and Stryker poured some more for him. When he had taken his drink, he pulled his bandana from his neck and wetting it he wiped around Waco's eyes and muzzle. Finally wiping his own face and neck, he put his wet hat back on his head and hung the canteen back on his saddle.

Shading his eyes, he picked up a dust cloud almost two or three miles distant. Scanning the horizon carefully he couldn't tell what it was at that distance, but he knew he had better be careful, the Apaches were still raiding about and some of the Cowboys from the Tombstone area often came up this way to rob and rustle.

Eastern Men

Making the decision to leave and try to stay against the sides of hills and rocky outcroppings, Stryker mounted and again took up the trail of the tracks he had been following.

Some time later, Stryker was traversing an open area keeping his eyes sharp in front of him. The tracks were leading almost in circles now and he found himself, more than once, almost in the same spot time and again. Reining in Waco he sat for a moment and thought. The first rifle ball came as a complete surprise and Waco jumped with all four legs. Spinning in the saddle Stryker saw six mounted Apaches at a full gallop comin up on him. Without taking time to think, he spurred Waco and sped off at a gallop. He knew Waco would never be able to sustain the run for long and he was going to have to come to a decision soon, but in the meantime, he gave Waco his head and felt the animal increase the speed.

There was nowhere to stop for cover, so when he felt he could; he reached for his Winchester carbine, pulling it from the carbine boot on his saddle. When it was free, he braced in his saddle throwing both feet forward and pulled back on his reins bringing Waco to a sliding stop while vaulting from the saddle at the same time. Slapping Waco on the rump with his Winchester, he dropped where he stood and got the carbine into firing position. Settling down, he jacked the lever of the carbine shoving a cartridge into the chamber and picked his target. Taking a breath, he squeezed and the rifle bucked into his shoulder. His target didn't go down though, so, cursing under his breath, he worked the lever again.

By now, the Apaches were trying to circle him, hoping for a chance to dart in for a kill. Indeed one tried just that and was rewarded with a .45 ball in his face as Stryker jerked around, pulled his pistol and fired. Returning his attention back to the other mounted men, the rifle balls were starting to find their range and were hitting very near to where he lay, totally exposed. By now, the Apaches were sure they had the advantage and were coming in closer. It was, to them, almost becoming a game with the prize laying directly in their grasp.

Stryker rolled to get a shot at one of the riders and felt the impact of the rifle ball on his right foot. Glancing down, he saw a hole in his boot and the pain was immediate and intense. So far he had only managed to hit the one Apache in the face and it wasn't enough to call them off. He knew they were not going to leave until he was dead. The only thing that was saving him at the moment was that he was flat on the ground and not a large target and these Apaches were not good shots.

For forty-five minutes the firing went back and forth but then came a new sound. Lying on the ground, Stryker could hear the pounding of hooves approaching. Taking the chance to lift his head higher, he caught site of two horses pounding his way. The Apaches caught sight of them as well and after throwing a few more shots at Stryker, turned their mounts and galloped off in another direction. Stryker watched a rider start the chase and fire a few shots at the fleeing Apaches from the rifle he held, but then he turned back and picked up the horse he had dropped off.

Pulling his horse up to a walk, he approached the now sitting Stryker and finally stopped in front of him.

"Lose somthin?" asked the Hunter.

"Just my pride, my horse and I think the big toe on my right foot," answered Stryker. "Seems ya found my horse, where'd you come from Mr. Hunter?" Stryker was trying to pull his boot off and the pain was shooting up his leg with each try.

"Waco ran straight back to us and I knew you were in trouble, that hurt a lot?" The Hunter dismounted and walked to Stryker. "Here, let me help, but don't go yellin at me if it hurts." He took hold of Stryker's boot and started pulling it off his mangled foot. When it came clear, he turned it upside down to drain the blood and squatted down to help pull off his sock. Stryker was right; the big toe was shot, but not off. Certainly shattered and it would require some healing time, but he would live. It would be one ugly toe, but he would live.

After rinsing out his boot, getting Stryker bandaged and ready to go, the Hunter helped Stryker onto his horse and then mounted Bandit. "You have problems, make sure ya tell me Jeff." The two men turned and started the hour-long ride back to Phineas and Sy Common. There were medical supplies there and the Hunter had purchased some of the same analgesics Mrs. Barnum had given him last year while his leg was healing. If nothing else, Stryker would have a story to tell. "Hell, we all need stories," he thought.

*****

Spats sat uncomfortably on a rock outside the circle of cavalry troopers. "We need to get someplace soon," he thought. "This desert is taking us apart." He glanced at Mr. O'Brien sitting quietly in the shade of a yucca plant, slowly tossing pebbles at alligator lizards dashing about around them. Spats rose to his feet stamping them to get circulation. "Be good to get to Tombstone eh Jamie?" he asked.

Eastern Men

Mr. O'Brien looked up at Spats and went back to tossing his pebbles not bothering to answer Spats or even acknowledge he had spoken.

Spats edged closer to Mr. O'Brien. Bending down, he eyed his friend closely. "Jamie, you alright?"

Mr. O'Brien exploded off his rock and slamming both his hands on Spat's chest, shoved him for all he was worth. Spats stumbled backwards and fell over a rock coming to rest on his back with one leg up over the rock.

"Am I alright?" spit Mr. O'Brien. "Am I alright? Yea Spats, I'm fucking great, that's why we're in the middle of the fucking desert, with nothing but what's on our backs, in a dust cloud that would choke a camel and no fucking idea where we are. Yea, Spats, I'm just fucking great!"

Spats picked him self up, not even bothering to brush himself off. Sitting on the rock he looked at Mr. O'Brien. "Ya had no call to do that Jamie, none. Yous been actin all crazy like for a while now and I was worryin is all."

Mr. O'Brien glanced at Spats and walked away to relieve himself without saying another word.

After the short noon break, the troopers were once again in the saddle with Spats and Mr. O'Brien bringing up the rear. They were both weary with the constant dust being kicked up by the sixty plus cavalry troopers and scouts riding in front of them. It was choking them and plainly serving to make Mr. O'Brien more irritable and uncomfortable and after awhile, he just seemed to drift into a deep sleep with his eyes open, barely able to stay on the swaying mount underneath him.

*****

"What the hell happened to you Jeff? asked Sy Common when the Hunter and Stryker rode up on them. He looked at Stryker's bloody bandaged foot dangling down on the side of his horse. "How bad is it?

The Hunter looked at Common and at Phineas. "Pretty mangled big toe, but he'll live," he said. "At least for a while he will," added the Hunter. Stepping down from Bandit, he motioned for Common to come over and help him get Stryker from his horse. Together the two men managed to get Stryker down and sitting on Common's saddle.

Phineas walked over and looked at Stryker's toe. "Looks bad all right, but I have seen worse in Brooklyn," said Phineas. Bending down to get a closer look he unwrapped the bandage the Hunter had put on. Looking up at the Hunter, he said, "It's not as bad as it seems, probably a lot more painful than damaged. Have you any laudanum?" he asked.

Eastern Men

"No laudanum," said the Hunter. "But we do have some analgesic I picked up in Tucson, that help?"

Phineas thought for a moment. "It will help some, but he will still have a pretty bad ache for awhile and he won't be wearing a boot for a while." Phineas stood and turned to the Hunter. "Analgesic in the packs?" he asked.

"Yessir, find my doctorin bag and it's in there." The Hunter turned back to Stryker. "Take it easy Jeff; Mr. Bellflower is bringin ya something for the pain."

Phineas returned carrying a paper packet and some bandaging material. Bending back down to Stryker, he poured some water into a coffee cup and added a white powder. Stirring it with his finger, he handed it to Stryker. "Drink it all down Jeff, all of it," he warned.

Stryker took the cup and put it to his lips and took a drink. Screwing up his nose, he pulled the cup from his lips. "That tastes something awful Mr. Bellflower," he said.

"All of it Jeff," said Phineas.

Pinching his nose like he did when young and having to drink castor oil, Stryker put the cup back to his mouth and took it down in two gulps. Handing the cup back to Phineas, Stryker shivered at the horrible taste in his mouth.

"I know it has a horrible taste, but it will help keep the pain down." Phineas leaned forward and poured some more water into the cup. Taking up a piece of muslin, he gently began washing to toe trying to remove all of the encrusted dried blood from the wound. When it was fairly clean, Phineas examined it carefully. Sitting back he announced. "He won't lose the toe, but it will be exceptionally sore for awhile."

The Hunter returned from the packs and handed Stryker a piece of anise candy. "Here," he said. "That'll take the bitter out." He turned to Phineas. "How long ya think he'll be outta the saddle Mr. Bellflower.?"

"Oh Hunter, you misunderstand. His foot will be sore, most certainly, but he will probably be able to ride tomorrow, if we can get his boot on." Phineas looked at the Hunter. "Does he have any spare socks?"

Stryker looked up at Phineas. "Why you askin him, Mr. Bellflower, they're my socks. Yea, I got some in my saddlebags." Stryker sat up a little. "Should be on the right."

Phineas walked to Stryker's saddle that Common had already put by the small campfire they had built and rummaged though Stryker's saddlebags until he came up with a thin pair of wool socks. They had the look of a lot of miles and rinsing, although he doubted whether these men ever washed their socks or underwear. Returning to the campfire, he handed the socks to Stryker. "See if you can get these on after I get you bandaged," he said. Gently and meticulously Phineas dressed the wound on Stryker's toe. When he was finished, it looked professional and the Hunter commented on it.

"That's a durn nice job Mr. Bellflower. It's almost like you was a doctor or something," said the Hunter.

"Medical school before I became a writer Hunter…I found writing paid far more, although the dangers matched the income I'm afraid." Phineas sat back. "There that ought to do it."

Stryker slipped the end of the sock over his toe then his foot. Things went well until his toe caught on a snag in the sock and he let out a yelp. Pulling the sock away from the toe he continued until it was all the way on his foot. "Seems ta be okay," he said. "But tomorrow is the boot. I ain't so sure about that."

The Hunter picked up the boot and looked at the hole in the toe. Examining the top and the sole where the ball had exited, he smiled. "You were lucky, Jeff, that ball coulda took yer foot off." Looking again at Stryker's foot and boot. "yer gonna throb some son, ain't no getting around it but we gotta move best we can. So's tomorrow, with or without that boot, yer getting a horse."

Eastern Men

Stryker looked at the Hunter with a sidelong glance. "Gonna be without the boot," he thought. "Damn sure is." He settled in as well as he could and waited for the throbbing to subside…

Eastern Men

SEVENTEEN

The cavalry patrol pulled into Fort Huachuca in mid afternoon. After they had called a halt and the troopers were given the orders to dismount, Al Seiber rode back to the two eastern men.

"Time ta get off them animals boys, this here is the end for you two." He turned and started back towards the front of the column when a voice called after him.

"You just gonna leave us here?" asked Spats. "Just leave us?"

"Just leave ya is right," answered Seiber. "You two are lucky we brung ya this far, now unass them horses."

"But we got no money, no way to get to Tombstone," said Spats. "Don't even know where it is from here. Hell, I don't even know if this is still Arizona, and yous are just gonna leave us here?"

"Look friend, you wanna go with us, enlist, otherwise get off them fuckin horses." Seiber again turned his horse towards the front of the column.

Spats turned to Mr. O'Brien. "It appears he's serious, Jamie. "Slowly he dismounted the weary horse and tied the leather lead to a hitch. Going to Mr. O'Brien's mount, he tied the lead to the hitch and touched Mr. O'Brien's leg. "You want me to help ya, Jamie?"

Mr. O'Brien glared down from on the horse for a full minute before finally speaking. "Leave me the fuck alone Mickey…just stay away."

Spats backed off and sat heavily on the step of a building staring at Mr. O'Brien, still perched atop the horse.

"Well, you gonna help me or just sit there, Mickey?" Mr. O'Brien turned to look at Spats sitting on the step. "Are you just going to sit there and ignore me?"

"That's exactly what I'm gonna do," replied Spats. "Exactly."

*****

The train moved slowly into the Tucson station pulled by a behemoth black engine, the black smoke flowing from the stack choking everything in it's path and causing people standing near the tracks to cover their mouths and noses. When it finally stopped with a squeal and a mighty thunderous belch of steam and more black smoke, a conductor stepped to the landing of the Pullman and put a whistle to his mouth. Blowing three times, he stuck his head back into the interior of the car and announced their arrival. "Tucson," he yelled. "Tucson, this is our final destination, everyone off!"

Eastern Men

One by one the passengers stepped down the steps to the raised boardwalk of the train station. Boots and shoes making thunking noises on the timbers as they moved into the station for departing schedules or walked to the end of the walk and stepped onto the dusty street.

The conductor made another sweep of the car and found a man sleeping in the rear of the car with his feet up on the seats across from him. Grabbing the man's foot he started shaking it to wake the slumbering figure in front of him.

Slowly the man came awake and stared at the conductor for a good thirty seconds while he shook the cobwebs from his head. When finally he remembered where he was, he spoke. "What do you want?" he asked.

"End of the line," said the Conductor. "Time ta get off the Pullman." The conductor stood with his hands on his hips waiting for the man to move from his seat. When the man didn't move, the conductor pushed the point. "Come on mister, ya gotta get yer ass off this Pullman, this train is goin inta the yard."

The man stood and gathered his satchel from the netting above him. Looking at the conductor, he put his Homburg on his head. "In Brooklyn, you would be walking a long way around me sir," he said moving down the aisle toward the open door.

"This here is Arizona Territory," the conductor called after him. "Ain't no one walks a long way around anyone out here."

*****

Stryker's foot throbbed incessantly and the analgesic Phineas had been giving him worked only when he was able to elevate his foot. Although he was able to get his leg across his saddle horn, it was not enough to abate the pain and Stryker rode all day with his foot throbbing horribly. Finally, toward the end of a long day in the saddle, the Hunter rode up to the group and reined in.

"How's the foot, Jeff?" he asked.

"Been hurtin pretty good, Mr. Hunter," replied Stryker. "Maybe by tomorra it'll ease a bit."

"By tomorrow we'll be in Contention City and you can see their doc, maybe get some laudanum for the pain." The Hunter stretched in his saddle and rubbed Bandit's neck. "Up the trail a bit is a nice spring, bout twenty, thirty minutes maybe. Good place for overnighting." He looked at Stryker. "You good for another little bit, Jeff?"

"Yessir, I'll make it good. Doncha worry about me none, but Mr. Bellflower," he paused for a moment, then continued. "Mr. Bellflower's been fidgetin a lot…meybe his fundament needs a little lookin after." Stryker looked over at Phineas sitting uncomfortably in his saddle.

The Hunter glanced at Phineas. "That right, Mr. Bellflower?"

Phineas moved his horse alongside of the Hunter. "To a degree Hunter, but the mention of Contention City tomorrow took some of the pain out." He smiled. "At least temporarily."

"It will be nice ta get off these mounts for a while I guess," piped in Sy Common. "Sides it ain't as much fun needlin Jeff with him hurtin and all."

Stryker smiled a wan smile at Common. "You ain't none too funny there Syrus…none at all." He looked at the Hunter. "If'n we're goin, Mr. Hunter, then let's git. I said I could make it good, I never said I wouldn't commence to screamin."

*****

The four men rode into Contention City just before noon. The hubbub was exactly as the Hunter remembered it when he and Jolly had been there and when he and Stryker had brought Sy Common in to the Contention Mine earlier in the year. The four halted in front of the train station and the Hunter dismounted. Stamping his feet, and bending at the waist to unlimber himself, he stepped onto the platform and into the cool interior of the station. There, behind the cage, in the same station, sat the same clerk he had spoken to in April of 1881. The clerk looked up from his ledger and studied the Hunter for a moment.

"Can I help you sir?" he asked. The clerk continued to study the Hunter. "I'm sorry sir, do I know you?"

The Hunter leaned on the counter and returned the look. Standing straight and pushing his hat back, the Hunter spoke. "I picked up the clothes left on the train a couple years back."

"Say, you're right!" responded the clerk. "That was the day Brocius and those other boys walked into town naked as jaybirds. Yessir, that was a sight all right." The clerk extended his hand. "R.G. Banning sir, and who am I addressing?"

The two men shook hands. "Folks just call me Hunter," the Hunter answered. "I'm lookin for yer doctor's office. Can you point me in the right direction?"

"Sure thing," answered the clerk. "Go out the door and turn right. When you get to Fourth Street, turn right again. The first set of stairs on your right is Doctor Wills' office."

Eastern Men

"I thank you, Mr. Banning," said the Hunter. He turned to leave the station when R.G. Banning called him back in.

"Say, Hunter? Whatever happened with those clothes I gave you?" asked Banning.

"They helped me find the man that was wearin em," Answered the Hunter. He waved at Banning and stepped back onto the platform. Untying his lead from the hitch, he mounted Bandit and turned them east on the street.

"The doctor's down on Fourth," said the Hunter. "Think you can take some stairs Jeff?"

"You just get me there, Mr. Hunter, I'll get up em for damn sure." Stryker grit his teeth at the thought of having to climb stairs, but the alternative wasn't any better, and he knew he had to have that toe looked at. Mr. Bellflower had been helpful, but Stryker needed a doctor.

In moments the four men were turning onto Fourth Street and coming to a halt next to the stairs. Tying their horses to the hitch in front of the gun shop, the Hunter and Sy Common helped Stryker up the stairs to the doctor's office. Opening the door, the men swung Stryker through the door and came in after him to steady him. Setting Stryker in a chair, the Hunter called out. "Doc, Doc Wills…you here?"

Presently and young well-dressed man came from the back into the office. "I'm Doctor Wills," he said. "Gentlemen, how may I be of service?"

"Well sir, this youngster here," the Hunter pointed at Stryker. "Sort a got hisself shot in the toe." He pointed at Phineas. "Mr. Bellflower here helped some, but I'm pretty sure he needs ta have a doc look at it."

Doc Wills kneeled in front of Stryker. "Let's just see that foot Mr., uh, Mr...."

"Stryker, Doc. Jeff Stryker," said Stryker. "Durn Apache musta been shootin at my head cause he sure as the dickens hit my foot." Stryker grinned broadly, pulled up his trousers and pushed his foot out.

The doctor gently peeled the bandage and checked out the toe. After a few moments of quiet grunts and noises, the doctor sat back on his haunches. "Well sir, I would say you got yourself one shot up toe all right, Mr. Stryker." The doctor got to his feet and walked to a cabinet against the far wall. Opening the doors, he took out bandages, assorted smaller items and a small bottle of a brown liquid. Returning to Stryker, he again squatted and started to work on Stryker's toe.

"You were lucky, Mr. Stryker, that bullet didn't take off your foot." He poured some clear liquid on a patch of gauze bandage and started swabbing Stryker's foot and toe. "Took off a nice chunk of meat, but it's not broken. It's gonna be sore for a couple more days, but I'll give you something for that." He finished cleaning the wound and lightly wound a dressing around the foot making sure there was a patch of gauze between his toes. "Might want to think about a slightly bigger boot and a little cleaner foot for a few days."

"Yessir, I sure will," responded Stryker.

"The doctor handed Stryker the small vial of brown liquid. "Take a small amount of this if the pain gets bad. It's laudanum, so be careful how much you take."

Stryker took the bottle and pushed it into his vest pocket. "Thanks Doc." He pulled some money from his trouser pocket. "What's the tariff?"

"Dollar fifty, today's price for big toes." The doctor grinned. "You just make sure you keep that toe down for awhile. No more gunshots, Mr. Stryker."

Stryker picked out a dollar-fifty from his fist and handed it to the doctor. "I plan on keepin a good holt on my other one Doc. I surely do." He struggled to his feet and grabbed the Hunter's shoulder. "Let's get them critters stabled, Mr. Hunter." The Hunter and Stryker shuffled towards the door. Turning to the doctor, the Hunter spoke.

Eastern Men

"Much obliged," he said. "I guess it coulda been worse, I guess he coulda got the whole toe shot off."

An hour later the four men had stabled, fed and watered their stock and were on the hunt for sit-down food that they didn't have to prepare. The Hunter turned down the street from the livery and stopped. Contention City had grown significantly since he was there last. The amount of restaurants, saloons and bawdy houses had increased along with the other businesses up and down the main thoroughfare. The bustle of the population had also increased with the addition of extra miners and workers at the hammer mill.

"That café' across the street looks promising," the Hunter said. Hitching up his gun belt, he started across the busy street.

The other three men followed and soon they were seated at a table by the window reading the Bill of Fare.

When they had ordered, Phineas spoke. "How far from here to Tombstone, Hunter?"

"Bout an hour or two's ride," answered the Hunter. "Kinda depends how fast we go, but we leave early we'll be in Tombstone long before noon. Last time I rode it was with Jolly, and we were following Curly Bill Brocius, he meandered all over the place. Stole my horse here in Contention." He settled back into his chair and stared out the window remembering when he and Jolly had been through Contention City at the start of the hunt for Thomas Hardy. Remembering their travels over the years, the arguments and the good deep conversations they had at times in the evenings when on the trail. Jolly had the knack of punching though the fog and getting straight to the point, a trait the Hunter respected as Stryker was blessed with it too.

Wiping the starting of a tear from his eye, he turned back to the others at the table. "I think when we are done here, I'm going to go back to the livery and take the rest of the day to ease the weariness from my bones."

"I think we all want that, Mr. Hunter," said Common. "We're all pretty tired of chasing all over the territory."

"Amen," said Phineas. "Amen to that, Mr. Common."

Eastern Men

EIGHTEEN

Whitey bent over the fire blowing carefully into it, trying to get the embers to build into a flame. It had been almost two days since their last fight and Whitey and Lenny were still not talking to each other. At times the silence was very loud as the looks flashed back and forth between them.

Lenny finished dressing the fat hare he had managed to catch and turned to Whitey, just as the flame came to life and started to snap and pop with the fresh mesquite fuel.

Whitey fed the fire finally turning to Lenny who was sitting just as morosely staring into the air before him. "Y'ever gonna talk ta me agin, Lenny? " he asked.

"Y'ever gonna let me do the fire and you traipse yer ass in the bushes looking for game?" asked Lenny. "Seems yer always the one lightin the fuckin fire and me that's shuckin through the cactus and scrub lookin fer food." He looked up at Whitey. "I can light a fire ya know."

"We got any a that money left at all?" asked Whitey skirting the issue. "Any?"

Lenny pushed his hand into his pocket and brought out a five dollar gold piece and a twenty-dollar note. Shoving it back into his pocket he said, "Twenty five dollars."

Eastern Men

"Well, at least that'll buy us a nice supper in Tombstone…that is unless Breckenridge sees us and throws us back outta town," said Whitey. "He was pretty plain he don't want ta see us around last time we was there."

"Yea, but with the Ghost gone and the Cowboys pretty much outta his hair, maybe he'll leave us be, we don't start any trouble." Lenny pushed the hare onto a stick and handed it to Whitey. "Just the same, we better stay clear a Mr. Breckenridge."

Whitey propped the rabbit over the fire and settled back watching it begin to sizzle and drop fat into the flames. He sat for a moment picking debris from his trousers and staring into the dirt. Finally turning to Lenny, Whitey cleared his throat and spat into the bushes. "What're we doin Lenny?" he asked. "What the fuck we doin?" He leaned forward and moved the rabbit off the direct flames. "Since Mr. Bellflower, we ain't had no luck at all. Hell we ain't had no luck since the fuckin Ghost." He stood up and stamped his feet. "Seems since them bandits robbed us in Mexico, we cain't do nuthin right no more."

"Not that we ever could," said Lenny under his breath.

"You say somethin, Lenny?" asked Whitey.

Eastern Men

"How long to Tombstone," said Lenny. "Think we shook that Richmond fella?"

"Couple days and from what I hear, don't think you can ever shake that Richmond fella," responded Whitey. "Ya think yer shed of him and you turn around, there he is." Whitey moved the rabbit again. And settled back onto his blankets. "Sure wish we had some beans and corn meal…sure do."

Sure wish we still had Mr. Bellflower's money is what I wish," said Lenny. "Twenty five fuckin dollars ain't gonna get us much. Not much at all."

Lenny lay back on his saddle and took in the territory around them. Mesquite was thick as was the cholla and brush cactus. Grease wood was scattered throughout in large clumps and they had to constantly pull their animals away as grease wood could be toxic to grazing animals unless they were acclimated to grazing it and their animals weren't. The rest of the ground was covered in a fine grass, dried from the sun but edible and they tried to keep their horses in the midst of it for fodder. Since the flood, they hadn't had proper food for themselves or their mounts and their horses were beginning to show the results on their rumps and chests.

Whitey leaned over and picked up the rabbit, pulling off a haunch, he then handed the rabbit to Lenny, which at that point was struggling to sit up. "Here, eat sumthin," he said.

Lenny took the hare and tore off the other haunch. Taking a bite, he chewed slowly. "I'm getting the fuck outta Arizona when we get to Tombstone. This just ain't fer me no more." He took another bite of rabbit. "Maybe California, I hear there's lotsa chances fer a fella there."

"California? Whatcha gonna do in California you can't do here in the territory?" asked Whitey.

"Not sweat so much maybe." Lenny finished the rabbit haunch and threw the bones into the brush. "Whitey, we ain't good at bounty huntin, we ain't good at bein guides or bandits neither. I suspect we ain't good at much but bein bad at things."

"Meybe so," said Whitey. Meybe so, but here in the territory we got the whole desert ta be bad in. I guess there's too many folks in California."

"I'm goin anyhow," said Lenny. "I'm goin ta that town, Los Angeles, and meybe be a hand on someone's ranch."

"You do that Lenny…you just do that, don't come runnin back ta me when ya can't get a stake at nuthin but bein a bandit agin," responded Whitey. "Just don't is all."

Eastern Men

Lenny lay down and rolled up in his blanket. "Tomorra mornin I'm gonna go into Tombstone and get a fresh horse and some supplies and start for California, that's what I am gonna do. I'll leave half the money for you at the Dexter Livery with Mr. Dunbar." He pulled his blanket up around his shoulders and settled onto his saddle. As he fell asleep, Lenny started dreaming of the warm sun and the cool breezes of Los Angeles, the wide-open places with no desert in sight.

*****

Spats turned around just as the fist came crashing into his face. He had gone into a bawdyhouse to see if there was any help to be had to get to Tombstone and instead had gotten into a scuffle with two cavalry troopers, beating the first one severely but not expecting the second one to explode like he just had. Recovering quickly, Spats moved into his fighting stance and began jabbing and weaving to stay away from the other man. Finally, throwing a one-two punch, his roundhouse lifted the trooper and threw him almost ten feet into the middle of the room. Spats stood breathing hard staring at the men sprawled on the floor.

"All I wanted was some help getting to Tombstone," he yelled at the figures. "Now look." He walked over to the first one and searched his pockets. Coming up with only three dollars and some change, he quickly searched the second one and found that trooper to be carrying almost forty dollars. Only taking twenty, Spats put the remainder of the money back into the trooper's pocket and went back outside where Mr. O'Brien still sat sullenly staring into the vast openness of the desert.

Spats knelt down slowly, paying attention to Mr. O'Brien's posture. "Jamie I got us some money to get to Tombstone. Come on, I think there is a stagecoach leaving pretty soon." Mr. O'Brien still sat staring. Spats grabbed his shoulders and shook him gently. "Come on Jamie, we have to go, the Army won't take it lightly that I beat two of their own…come on…lets go!" he shouted.

Slowly Mr. O'Brien stood and quietly replied to Spats. "Fine," he said. "Fine, you lead."

The two men made their way to the stage depot and bought two tickets for Tombstone. Now it was a waiting game, they had to get out of Huachuca before the two troopers came to and reported the beating to their officers. Fortunately the stage was on-time and came rolling in from Benson disgorging it's passengers and taking on a new team before the final leg of their trip to Tombstone.

Eastern Men

Finally, twenty minutes later, Spats and Mr. O'Brien were seated in the rolling coach in route to Tombstone and, they hoped, Phineas Bellflower.

*****

The ride into Tombstone was miserable for the man from Brooklyn. Mike McManus was used to comfortable carriages as transportation, not bouncing along in a rickety stagecoach, eating dust and smelling the people sittin next to and across from him.

When he had arrived in Benson on the train, he was told that there would not be a train to Contention City for another day. Fuming, he had gotten the information about the stagecoach and had stomped across the street to the stage depot and bought a ticket. Now he was stuck in the rolling abomination, sweating profusely and having to endure the various body odors of those seated around him.

The man across from him wore a large brimmed hat, a vest, purple silk bandana and a big revolver on his hip. He was staring at McManus with a bemused smile on his face. When McManus couldn't take it any longer, he spoke to the man.

"Something about me amuse you sir?" McManus asked and stared hard at the man.

Eastern Men

"No sir, not a bit. Seems ta me you are mighty fidgety though, like we bother you," he waved his hand around at the other passengers. "You got a way about ya that tells me ya think yer a pretty important gent." The man pushed his hat back on his head. "That's all," he said.

"There are some that think I'm a very important man," said McManus.

"Not in this coach," replied the man across from him. "Probly not in this territory neither," he furthered. "Thinkin yer too big around these parts gets ya killed. Ain't no one around here can't be killed. You can make bank on that." The man adjusted his seat and looked back at McManus. "You best be rememberin that when ya get to Tombstone, folks there don't go toleratin high flutin mucky mucks." The man settled into his seat, pulled his hat down and drifted off to sleep.

"High flutin mucky muck my ass," thought McManus.

*****

The Hunter pulled his cinch tight and mounted Bandit. Leaning over he picked up the lead to the mule and turned his horse towards the other men. "All set?" he asked. "Jeff, you good?"

Eastern Men

"Yessir, Mr. Hunter," replied Stryker. "Foot ain't hurtin so much now, and with a small swig a this laudanum, don't hardly bother me 'tall"

"Good, good." The Hunter turned back to Common. "Syrus, watch our rear. It would be a shame to have anyone come up from behind us…not that I think they will." He stood in his stirrups and sat back down adjusting himself. "Gentlemen, let's go." All four men squeezed their mounts and started on their last leg into Tombstone.

Two and a half hours later they were sitting on a hill outside the Toughnut mine, looking down on the bustling mining camp of Tombstone, AT. The four men looked on as the streets of Tombstone appeared to teem with people and rigs. Before them lay Toughnut Street and beyond that Allen and Fremont Streets busily going on with everyday life.

Slowly the riders made their way down the hill and onto Goose Flats. Turning their horses, they walked them to Fifth Street then to Allen and stopped them at the hitch in front of the Oriental Saloon. Sitting for a moment, the Hunter stretched in his saddle before stepping down from Bandit. Unbuckling his bridle, he slipped it from Bandit's mouth and hung it on his saddle horn. Untying the lead to his halter, he wrapped it around the hitch with a small loop and left the rest hanging. Walking around Bandit, he pulled his Winchester from the rifle boot and turned to the others.

"If ya ain't been here before, your weapons have to be turned in while we are in town. They'll take them right here at the Oriental," said the Hunter. I don't know about the rest of ya, but I'm goin in for a drink…y'all comin?"

To the man, the other three grabbed what weapons they had and followed the Hunter into the cool interior of the Oriental Saloon.

Walking in the door, the Hunter turned to the left and walked to the bar. Putting his weapons on the bar, he cleared his throat and waited for the barman to turn towards him.

"Yessir," said the barman.

"Now there's a sorry lot if I ever seen one," came a voice from the back of the room.

The Hunter turned and found himself looking directly at Buck Simpson and Mingo Perez.

"Now it seems ta me that that youngster there with that grizzled old fart oughta be gettin smart enough to figure out he ain't worth a toss." Buck grinned a wide grin. "Mr. Hunter…what brings you to Tombstone?"

"What the hell happened to Stryker's foot?" chimed in Mingo.

Eastern Men

The Hunter walked to the table. "What are you two doing here? Isn't it time for a round-up?"

"Done. Delivered the horses to Fort Bowie Tuesday. Mingo thought a short trip to Tombstone would be kinda sweet and then we'll head back to the 'A'." Buck took a drink of beer and put his mug back on the table. "A course, if ya want us to skedadle now, I'm guessin we probly could."

The Hunter eyed the two men. "Nah, go ahead, get some fun in before you go back." He turned and walked back to the bar. "How about beers for all my friends?"

The barman turned and grabbed some mugs, filling them and sliding them to the men. The Hunter reached into his trousers and pulled out some rumpled paper currency and slid it to the barman. "How about storing these weapons here?"

"No problem sir." The barman took up the various weapons the men had deposited on the bar and stashed them underneath. "Be here when you leave," he said.

The four men made their way to Buck and Mingo's table. "Buck, Mingo, this here is Mr. Phineas Bellflower, late of Brooklyn, New York and Chicago. The other one is Syrus Common, late of the Contention mine and a current neer-do-well," the Hunter said. "Mr. Bellflower, Syrus, these are two lazy shirkers that just happen to work for me on the Bar-A.

Eastern Men

The ugly one is Buck Simpson, ranch top hand, the other one is Mingo Perez, ranch foreman and the best damn horse trainer this side of the Rockies."

The men shook hands all around and sat at the table.

Buck sat forward in his chair. "So Mr. Hunter, what brings you to Tombstone?" He looked at Stryker's foot. "And Jeff, what did happen to your foot?"

"Some durn Apaches jumped me down to the Huachuca's. Kept me ta ground for near an hour. Took a rifle ball through my boot," said Stryker. "It's healin but sure did hurt there for awhile until the doc in Contention patched it up and give me some laudanum."

"Ya get em?" asked Buck. "Damn Apaches are raidin all over, even down to The Traces."

"Got one, the others stayed runnin and outta range mostly," said Stryker. "Been to the 'J'?" he asked.

"We's there when we was drivin them nags ta Bowie. Billy Drewer is doin a bang up job and that new hand, what's his name, Ingalls, he's breakin and gentlin the horses afore they get to Mingo…seems ta know what he's doin all right," responded Buck.

"Mr. Jolly sure didn't deserve that," said Stryker. "Sure didn't. I wish I coulda caught up ta that Ghost feller 'fore he got to the 'J'."

Eastern Men

The Hunter leaned forward and looked at Stryker. "Jolly lived his whole life for just that time Jeff, ain't no sense beatin yerself up over it, wasn't your fault and nuthin you coulda done about it…Jolly wouldn't a had it no other way," said the Hunter. "Sides, some folks just don't mind dyin, specially if they done everything they wanted." He took a large drink of his beer and thought for a moment. "I think his only real regret was the Kid, not knowin him before he did."

"Jolly was sumthin, no doubt," said Mingo. "There was just sumthin about him that folks couldn't leave alone…sumthin right and pure."

"Pure devil, y'ask me," Chimed in Buck. "Knew his stuff about minin though…and a fair rancher too even though he hated it." Buck sat for a moment then continued. "Seems all he really cared about was that damn mesa."

The Hunter stood raising his beer glass. "To Jolly Goodman," he said. "To a friend, compadre, a confidant and the biggest pain in my ass ever!"

The rest of the men stood and raised their glasses in unison. "To Jolly Goodman!" they exclaimed. At once all of them drained their beers and slammed the glasses on the table.

Eastern Men

"Hey boys, them glasses cost money," said the barman.

Sy Common and Phineas Bellflower looked at each other and simultaneously mouthed, "Who's Jolly Goodman?"

NINETEEN

The stage from Huachuca rattled into Tombstone with a flourish. The driver, knowing he had some room took the horses into a run and slid to a stop outside the Wells Fargo office. With the dust swirling in the air, people began disembarking from the coach until Spats and Mr. O'Brien stepped into the dusty street. Dusting off their tattered clothes, Spats turned slowly and took in all that Tombstone had to offer. Turning to Mr. O'Brien, Spats hocked and spat into the street.

"This sure isn't what I expected," said Spats. "Isn't nuthin here." He walked to a man at the depot shoving freight around. "Can you tell me where we are? This Tombstone?" asked Spats.

The man stood and stared at Spats for a moment before he straightened up and pointed to the sign hanging over the door which read…"Tombstone, AT, Elev: 4600 Feet" "Ain't nowhere else friend. I s'ppose it could be Contention City but that ain't spelt with a 'T'." The man went back to his freight with a chuckle.

Spats thought for a moment and decided it wasn't worth it and let the snide comment go. Turning on his heel, he walked back to Mr. O'Brien. The two men turned down

190

Eastern Men

Fifth Street and the world opened up to them. Allen Street was the center of the Tombstone camp and held everything from general stores, saloons, miner's supplies, dance halls and the newly opened Bird Cage Theatre. People were milling about going about their business as Spats and Mr. O'Brien stepped around the corner to the boardwalk and took in everything Tombstone had to offer. Stopping at the open door of the Alhambra Saloon, Spats pulled Mr. O'Brien inside and walked to the bar.

"Afternoon gents, what can I getcha?" asked the barman.

"Your beer cold?" asked Spats.

"You bet, we got one a the best ice houses in the territory right here in Tombstone," replied the barman. "Ice cold beer, and free lunch to the patrons of the Alhambra." The barman pointed to a table at the far end of the bar stacked with bread and meats. A small Mexican boy stood next to the table and waved a fan over, what appeared to be potato salad and coleslaw.

"How about a couple cold beers, and a couple of short glasses of anything Irish, " said Spats.

"Comin right up. You gents just help yourselves to the vittles." The barman turned and poured two beers placing them on the bar and picked up a bottle of Irish whiskey, pouring two short glasses, placing them both on the bar as well. "That'll be six bits."

Spats dug into his pockets and counted our seventy-five cents, placing it on the bar. "Thank you," said Spats as he reached for the whiskey. "Come on Jamie, drink up, it'll make ya feel a bit better."

Mr. O'Brien took up a glass and brought it to his lips. He took a small drink and set it back on the bar, staring at the floor, almost unmoving. "We're never going to see Brooklyn again Mickey," he finally said.

"Sure we will Jamie," replied Spats. "In fact, why don't we wire Mr. McManus for funds, and let's get ourselves back to Brooklyn. We can just tell him we never found Bellflower, which wouldn't be a total lie." Spats took a large drink of his beer. "Besides, he added. "We got nothin left us." Spats turned towards the food and walked over to get something to eat.

"Mr. McManus isn't that big a fool Mickey, but you may have something there." Mr. O'Brien drank the last of his whiskey and then took a drink of his beer wiping his mouth with what was left of his sleeve. He thought a minute, a little more animated now with the prospect of getting out of the hated territory of Arizona and the desert. Even at forty six hundred feet, it was still hot and dusty and miserable for the two eastern men.

Spats walked back over toting a makeshift sandwich and chewing. "Hell, this is the most I've had to eat in a couple days, since the flood at least," he said. "Yous should try some Jamie, it'll make ya feel better."

Mr. O'Brien walked to the table and made himself a small sandwich, taking a huge bite and chewing slowly. When he finally could say something he spoke again. "I feel fine Spats, just fine. Didn't I see a telegraph office down the street?" he asked. For the first time in days, Spats saw a light in his friend's eyes.

*****

The six men sat at the table talking of Apache attacks, they way they had found Phineas, all about Syrus Common and then the Hunter heard about the Bar-A. Heard about Charlie and Clara and the girls. The new outbuildings they had built, and the expansion of the range they had to make to accommodate the rising amount of horses they were getting requests for.

When the Hunter turned toward the bar to motion the barman for more beer, he saw a very tall, very large black man come into the Oriental He was dusty from head to foot so much he appeared to be gray and was dressed in range clothing sporting a hat with a huge wide brim and short crown. Unbuckling his gun belt, he hoisted it up on the bar, dusted himself with his hat and leaned forward ordering a beer. The same moment, from the corner of his eye, the Hunter saw two men rise from the rear of the room and start to walk to the front of the bar, one on each side of the man. When they reached him, the larger of the two leaned into the man and spoke loud enough for everyone in the bar to hear.

"Yer a big buck ain't ya boy?" the man asked him. "Ya wanna broom yerself off, do it outside, in fact, we don't wantcha in here noway."

The black man ignored him and took a large drink of his beer, carefully putting it back on the bar.

The second man grabbed the man's arm and spun the big man towards him. "A white man talks to you boy, you answer him savvy?" he asked.

The big man looked at the second man and then over at the first one. "Yassuh, I hears ya," he said and returned to drinking his beer.

The first man, got back into the man's face sneering. "You deaf nigger, I just tolt ya we didn't want ya in here…"

With lightning speed, the big man grabbed his beer and hit the first man square in the face with it, turning, he grabbed the second man by his shirt and the crotch of his trousers and lifting him, he walked to the door and threw him backwards into the street. Turning on his heel, he walked back to the bar. "Scuse me suh, I'll be needin another beer," he said. "This one's broke."

"Baily, I'm buyin it...doncha even think about it mister," said Mingo.

The man turned around and looked at the men sitting at the table. "Much obliged suh," he said. When his beer got there, he picked it up and drank it down in one long pull. Putting the glass on the bar, he turned to leave.

"Hey! Come join us," said Mingo. "We got plenty a room and, unlike some others, we got manners."

The man stared at the table and the six men, finally shrugging his huge shoulders and walked to the table where Mingo had brought another chair and everyone had made room. Just as the man was about to sit, the second man came crashing back into the bar waving a piece of flat iron, charging right for the big man. With a swing of his arm and balled up fist, the big man hit the running man square in the chest driving the air from his lungs and knocking him back through the door and back into the street.

When he was sure he would have no further trouble from either one of the two men, the big man turned and sat at the table. "Some folks are just downright rude, " he said.

"Surely hate that word suh…folks got no call ta use that word jest cause they thinks they can."

The Hunter watched silently as Mingo talked to the man. "Names Mingo, Mingo Perez. This here ugly one is Buck Simpson, over there is Mr. Richmond, next ta him is Jeff Stryker, then that's Mr. Bellflower and last is Syrus Common, and you are?" he asked.

"Folks jest call me Bountiful Jim, " he answered. "I ain't from nowhere particular and ain't goin nowhere particular neither, no suh, I surely ain't."

The barman brought fresh beer for everyone and Bountiful Jim picked up his glass. "I thank ya for the kindness, suh."

"No need for thanks…and I ain't no sir, Jim. I'm Mingo…jest plain Mingo," said Mingo. He looked over at the Hunter, and almost imperceptibly the Hunter nodded to him. "I got use on the ranch for a good hand. You a good hand Jim?"

"Yes suh. Been to the Pecos across the Red and Canadian inta Kansas a whole lotta times," He looked at Mingo and continued. "I've rode point, drag and flank so often all I kin see sometimes when I sleep is cows."

Eastern Men

"We ranch horses. How're ya with horses?" asked Buck. "Seems we kin get all the cow hands we want, but horsemen are few and hard ta come by."

"I loves horses suh, I gots a way with em all right," answered Jim. "Yes suh, I surely do."

"Mr. Bountiful, I'm curious as to how you came up with the name 'Bountiful Jim'," asked Phineas. "It seems a bit odd."

Bountiful Jim eyed Phineas for a moment. "Well suh, on a drive ta Dodge in '78, I was in the bushes relievin myself and another drover walked up askin if'n I had the papers. When I got up ta button my drawers, he caught a look at my pod and when I came in from ridin herd that evening they was all callin me 'Bountiful Jim'...I reckon they all thought it was funny and it jest stuck is all."

The others at the table sat and listened. One by one they started laughing until all seven men were laughing and saying 'Bountiful'.

"Not me," said Buck. I'd be known as 'Pitiful Buck'." The table again exploded with laughter.

When things quieted down a little, the Hunter turned to Mingo. "Mingo, We have to get Mr. Bellflower to the stage depot. You leavin today?" asked the Hunter.

"Yessir, soon as I kin get this sorry excuse for a top hand off a his ass..." Mingo didn't finish the thought but turned to Jim. "You comin Jim?

Bountiful thought it over for a moment. "Your other hands gonna take to it all right?" asked Bountiful. "It's already hard fer a colored man, seems they don't want em out here as much as Texas."

Stryker looked at Bountiful. "You from Texas Jim?" he asked.

"Why yessuh Mr. Jeff. Down ta Waco way. Worked the Five Mountain fer Mister..."

"Furley," said Stryker. "Mr. Furley at the Mountain ...known it my whole life." Stryker stood and pushed out his hand. "Honor ta know ya Jim."

The two men shook hands. "Yes suh Mr. Jeff, a real pleasure," said Bountiful. "A real pleasure, Mr. Jeff, it surely is." Bountiful looked at Mingo and Buck. "I reckon I'll be goin with ya Mr. Mingo. I ain't got no horse though, mine died comin in from Lordsburg, but if you kin stand me a mount, you kin take it from my wages."

"No rider from the 'A' goes horseless Jim, we'll go down to the Dexter or OK Corrals and get ya a mount. You got a seat too?" asked Mingo.

Eastern Men

"Yes suh, right outside this door here, left it there comin in, bridle and blanket too, if'n that feller I threw out ain't ruint it by now." He smiled with a broad grin. "Sure looked funny flyin out that door like he done. Yes suh, he surely did"

Eastern Men

TWENTY

An hour later Buck, Mingo and Bountiful Jim were on their way back to the Oro Valley and the Hunter and his group were watching them ride westward towards Boot Hill and the trail through The Traces.

About five miles outside of Tombstone, Mingo turned to Bountiful. Thinking for a moment, he finally spoke. "Jim, you don't really talk like that do you?" he asked.

Bountiful reined in his horse and turned to Mingo. "Nah, it's jest white folk mostly seem ta be more comfortable with it."

"Well, not at the 'A'," said Mingo. "We're just comfortable that a man gives us a days work for a days pay, is honest and gives us loyalty as long as he is working for us."

Bountiful, adjusted himself in his saddle. A moment later, he was grinning ear to ear. "Yes suh, I will, I surely will." Bountiful turned his horse and again urged his mount in the direction of the Bar-A and the Oro Valley, a little northwest of Tucson.

Eastern Men

Buck leaned over and clapped Mingo on the back and both men urged their horses forward trotting to catch up with Bountiful Jim.

*****

Michael McManus stepped from the coach and started brushing the dust from his clothes. The taste of dirt in his mouth was distracting and the grit in his hair and on his face and hands was unacceptable for a man such as Michael McManus. Finally, getting some sense of comfort, McManus looked around him at the businesses and stage depot of Fremont Street. Catching sight of a man sweeping the steps in front of the depot, McManus walked over to him, still sweeping dust from his clothing.

"Excuse me, I am to assume I am in Tombstone?" McManus watched the man sweep.

Finally when the man stopped sweeping. He stood up and pointed at the sign hanging on the front of the Depot which read, "Tombstone, AT, Elev: 4600 Feet". The man chewed for a moment then spat a large glob of chewing tobacco juice close to McManus' feet. "Getting so's a man can't complete a task without a yahoo botherin him. Second time taday somebody cain't read." He leaned on his broom and looked at McManus. "This here is the municipality of Tombstone, Arizona Territory, and this, this here is the

Eastern Men

Wells Fargo stage depot, and I am the clerk to the fuckin stage line…now if'n y'all wanna know where to go from here, jest you walk up that street right there to Allen Street and leave me the fuck alone." The clerk went back to his bowed brooming of the steps with nothing further to say.

McManus pulled his coat down and straightened his tie and turned up the directed street to find Allen Street and, and hopefully, Spats Melloy and Mr. O'Brien. "I'll pick up my bags later," he thought to himself. He also thought maybe, just maybe Phineas Bellflower wouldn't be far. "That would be nice, real nice."

*****

After learning the next stage out was in the afternoon, the following day, the Hunter deposited Mr. Bellflower into the Grand Hotel for the night and walked back to the camping spot they liked.

Syrus Common had already left town, headed for New Mexico Territory hoping his prospects there would be better than he had experienced in Arizona. The men shook hands all around as Common mounted his horse and picked up the lead of his pack mule. "It's been an honor Mr. Hunter. I want ta thank ya for the help when I needed it, and for the kindness shown me."

Eastern Men

Stryker looked up at Syrus. "You take care Syrus, them Apaches are still runnin around out there somewheres." He patted Common's horse's neck. "You mind this mount, don't go ridin him ta ground. Take 'er slow and easy and he'll last all the way to the Rockies I'm thinkin."

"Good-bye Jeff, it's been good sharin the trail with you and Mr. Hunter. Tell Mr. Bellflower good-bye for me too when ya see him, would ya?" Syrus straightened in his saddle and gave his horse a little squeeze. Turning in his saddle, he gave a small wave to the Hunter and Stryker as he turned up Fifth Street and out of sight.

"Nice fella," said Stryker as he watched him leave.

"He was that," responded the Hunter. "How about something to eat we ain't fixed?" asked the Hunter.

"How about," said Stryker. The two men started up out of the arroyo and made their way to Nellie Cashman's restaurant.

*****

Whitey Wellford stared down at the town of Tombstone. Grateful they had finally made it, they were now going to have to try to evade deputy Billy Breckinridge as long as they could. With their funds all but gone, they had enough for a meal and an evening's drinking before they were once again forced to take up the robber's trail. Turning to Lenny he pulled his hat from his head and scratched his head. "What if that fuckin Hunter is here Lenny?" he asked.

"So what?" said Lenny. "We ain't done nuthin ta him. He should be leavin us peaceful."

Whitey thought for a moment. "Yea," he finally said. "But Mr. Bellflower was with him, that means maybe he's here too…that could be trouble," he said.

"I keep forgettin about him," said Lenny. He reached down and scratched his leg. "So what if he is? Think he'll go to the fuckin law?"

Whitey rubbed his jaw and thought for a moment. "Nah, too fuckin proud I'm guessin." He gathered his reins and mounted his emaciated mount. "Them eastern assholes always are thinking they can take care a their own shit till the likes a us proves em wrong."

"The likes a us Whitey? What you mean?" asked Lenny. "I ain't never thought a us as the likes a us." He thought for a while. "I jest think a us as us is all."

Whitey turned to Lenny. "Get on yer horse, Lenny…I swear, you would try the fuckin preacher man." Whitey shook his head and started down the hill towards Tombstone.

*****

The telegraph operator took the written message from Mr. O'Brien and read it. "This it then?" he asked. He started

Eastern Men

counting the words. "Gonna be almost three dollars…up front." He looked up at Mr. O'Brien. "Two dollars-ninety in fact."

Mr. O'Brien looked over at Spats for the money. Spats dug into his trouser pocket and fished out the cash, which totally depleted the money they had left.

"That's it, Jamie, yous got it all." Spats stepped back from the counter and readied to return out to the boardwalk.

Mr. O'Brien handed the operator the money, thanked him and the two men walked back out into the Arizona sunshine.

Sitting on a small bench in front of a haberdashery, the two men watched the activity in the street. Spats elbowed Mr. O'Brien and nodded towards the west at two figures riding very sorry looking animals and walking slowly down the street. Slowly the two riders approached when they caught sight of Spats and Mr. O'Brien sitting on the boardwalk.

"Well looky here, Whitey, if'n it ain't them two eastern Brooklyn scudders we helped out a ways back." Lenny reined in his horse in front of Spats and Mr. O'Brien.

Spats turned to Mr. O'Brien. "Well look here, Jamie, if it isn't the two desert assholes we run into a while ago."

Eastern Men

Whitey reined in his horse and turned him towards the boardwalk. "Appears they made it outta the desert, Lenny."

Mr. O'Brien stood up and walked to the edge of the boardwalk staring at the two riders. "You may think you are humorous gentlemen, but believe me when I say, under different circumstances, you would not have that stupid smirk on your faces."

Whitey looked at Mr. O'Brien, over to Spats and back to Mr. O'Brien. Adjusting in his saddle, he leaned forward and spoke slowly with a low voice. "Well, we ain't under different circumstances, we ain't without the price of a meal, nor the coin ta stand fer a drink a whiskey," he said. "Leastways we got our mounts, as bad as they are, got our guns and hats. You ain't got but what's on yer frames."

Whitey and Lenny finally dismounted and started down the street towards the Dexter Livery. Stopping a moment later, Whitey turned around and looked at the sorry two people standing on the boardwalk in front of the store. Turning back to Lenny he again started down the street. "I ever get that bad just shoot me, Lenny," he said.

Together the two men walked their horses to the livery.

Eastern Men

TWENTY ONE

When the Hunter and Stryker had finished their meals, they made their way back to their camp and made some coffee. While the coffee cooked on the fire, Stryker went to check the animals. Lightly graining them and watering them, he returned to the camp laying on his bedroll. Thinking for a while with his eyes closed, he finally raised up on an elbow.

"Mr. Bellflower is a strange duck ain't he, Mr. Hunter?" Stryker asked.

The Hunter looked at Stryker and rubbed his chin. "Maybe not so strange for Brooklyn or Chicago, but he sure has some strange notions for the Sonora all right," he said. Leaning back against his saddle, he rolled one of his infrequent cigarettes. Lighting it and taking a big puff, he sucked it in and exhaled with a light whooshing noise. "It's hard goin places we ain't ready for, Jeff. Be like us goin to Chicago or New York, we ain't ready for it and not used to it. Be like ducks outta the water." The Hunter leaned forward and pulled the pot away from the direct flames.

"Yessir, I get that. I got no notion to go there anyhow," said Stryker. "Took me long enough ta get used to this territory, got no use on getting used to a big city, none at

Eastern Men

all." Getting to his knees, he leaned forward and poured some coffee into his cup then leaned back, his back against his saddle. "I wonder what happened to them fellas huntin Mr. Bellflower?" Stryker took a drink of the hot liquid. "What did he call them, Spats and, somebody, Mr. ...ah, somebody."

"O'Brien," answered the Hunter. "Mr. O'Brien." He poured some coffee for himself and the Hunter leaned back as well. "Probably didn't make it, Jeff."

"My brain ain't sayin that, Mr. Hunter," replied Stryker. My brain is sayin them fellas are safe somewhere." He took a drink of coffee and set the cup next to him on the blanket. "But, yer probly right anyhow." Stryker laid his head on his saddle, his toe aching from too much walking and his hip hurting from limping.

The Hunter put his cup down and in the gathering darkness breathed a big sigh. His thoughts went to Jolly and the Circle-J. "I have to go there," he thought. "Pretty damn soon...Billy Drewer will be needin some help." Three minutes later the Hunter and Stryker were both sound asleep.

*****

Phineas walked through the lobby of the Grand Hotel unable to sleep. It was now past nine in the evening and although he had tried, he was no closer to sleeping and so he was going to take a stroll around Tombstone. Walking out the door, he caught sight of two men sitting on a bench in front of a clothing store. He squinted in the darkness. They were familiar even in the dark, Spats and Mr.. O'Brien. "Of all places," thought Phineas. He turned back into the hotel, slightly panicked, and went downstairs to the bar.

"What kin I getcha?" asked the barman. "Got a full bar."

"Got Scotch?" asked Phineas. "I would love to have a drink of Scotch." He stood in front of the bar shaking like a leaf. He hadn't been this frightened in a long while, not even when they were fighting the Apaches, but seeing Spats and Mr. O'Brien jolted him to his core.

"We got Scotch," said the barman. "From Scotland too, none a this fake Kentucky shit for us, no sir." He flipped his bar towel over his shoulder. "How about Glenlivet, I hear it's pretty good, for them a you that likes it anyhow." He reached behind him and took a bottle from the back bar. Pouring a goodly amount into a glass, he pushed it to Phineas. "Six bits," he said.

Phineas reached into his pocket and took out the paper money the Hunter had given him earlier. Passing a dollar to the barman, he eagerly accepted the glass of whiskey. Picking up the glass, he held it under his nose for a second before turning the glass upside down and poured the whiskey into his mouth. Swallowing, he felt the Scotch start the burn to his stomach and allowed the glow to start over his body. Putting the glass back on the bar, he motioned to have it filled again, which the barman happily complied. Again Phineas slid the barman a dollar and again, he downed the liquor in one gulp.

"I never seen a fella turn down Scotch like that mister," said the barman. "Most folks sip it slow."

"I'm not most folks," responded Phineas. "Again please."

For the third time the barman filled Phineas' glass. But this time, Phineas did sip it, having already calmed his jangled nerves.

"Someone after you mister?" asked the barman.

Phineas looked up at the barman. "Why do you ask?

"Well sir, ya come in here shakin like a leaf, that's why I asked," said the barman. "Sides, yer suckin down Scotch whiskey like it's nuthin."

"It is something," said Phineas. "It's damn good Scotch."

*****

Whitey pulled the saddle from his horse, using the saddle blanket to wipe the animal down. When he was finished, he threw the saddle on a saddletree and hung the bridle from the saddle horn. Turning to Lenny, he watched Lenny finish with his horse. "We buy grain fer them too?" he asked.

Lenny looked at Whitey as he hung his bridle on his saddle horn. "Yea, cost us another dollar too." Pulling his bandana from his neck, he wiped the sweat from his face and neck then moved over to the grain and scooped two large scoops per animal and dumped them in front of the horses making sure they also had water and hay. "Two dollars at the livery, damn, no wonder them livery owners always have bank script." Walking to the street Lenny thought for a moment then turned to Whitey. "How do you suppose them two assholes got ta Tombstone, Whitey?" He scratched his head. "Probly same as us I guess."

"They didn't look like they was in good shape for sure," said Whitey. "How much we got left, Lenny?"

Lenny pulled money from his pocket and counted it out. "Twenty three dollars and some small change. We still gotta eat too."

"We kin eat cheap enough, we gotta save enough fer some whiskey though…God, I would love a drink a whiskey," said Whitey. "A whole fuckin bottle maybe."

Eastern Men

Both men crossed the street. Looking for a diner, or, better yet, a saloon with free food. They stopped in front of the Grand Hotel and looked around.

"Breckenridge likely ta come in here?" Lenny jerked his thumb towards the door of the hotel.

"Doubtful," answered Whitey. "Doubtful."

Whitey and Lenny turned into the Grand hotel and asked the desk clerk where they could find the saloon.

The clerk looked at them and responded. "This is the Grand, gentlemen. We do not have a saloon, we have a nice bar downstairs."

"We have a nice bar downstairs," mimicked Lenny. "Well, where the fuck is the nice bar downstairs?" Lenny leaned into the clerk.

"There are spiral stairs right behind you sir. You will find the bar at the bottom." The clerk stepped back; the aromatic assault was starting to get to him. The two cowboys were filthy and what's more, stank fiercely.

Whitey and Lenny turned and walked to the staircase going down into the floor and began to go down step by step.

When Lenny got almost to the bottom he glanced in front of him and there, standing at the bar, stood none other than Phineas Bellflower, busily downing a glass of some sort of liquor.

Eastern Men

Lenny immediately stopped and started backing up the stairs immediately running into Whitey.

"Hey, what the fuck!" yelled Whitey. "Just what are you fuckin doin?"

Lenny put his finger to his lips. "Shhhsh," he said. In a whisper he leaned towards Whitey. "Mr. Bellflower's in there."

Whitey looked surprised and backed up the stairs to the lobby of the Grand. When Lenny got back up to the first floor, both men turned and walked out the front doors to the boardwalk.

"Jesus, Mr. Bellflower…now how do you suppose…" Lenny said out loud. "Fuck, Whitey, we gotta stay low, if Mr. Bellflower finds us, he's sure ta turn us inta the sheriff."

With that, Whitey and Lenny ducked off the boardwalk and went directly to the livery to spend the night with their horses away from a prying lawman's eyes.

TWENTY TWO

The morning broke clear and cool. Spats woke on the bench in front of the haberdashery trying to straighten out his torso. In the doorway of the Western Union office, Mr. O'Brien was going through the exact process after having slept in the doorway propped against the frame.

Spats and Mr. O'Brien were on their way to find a privy when the telegraph operator came out of the office and ran right into Mr. O'Brien.

"Oh sir, I'm glad you're here," he said. "I finally got word back from New York. Seems no one can locate your Mr. McManus. No funds have been sent."

Mr. O'Brien looked at the telegrapher and at Spats, and then he sat heavily on the boardwalk. "I told you Mickey, there is no leaving this god forsaken shit hole." He sighed heavily. "I'll die here, I just know it."

"Don't give up Jamie, yous got a lot left. We'll make out, we always do." Spats knelt down next to Mr. O'Brien and put his arm on his shoulder. "We'll make out Jamie." Spats looked up at the telegrapher. "Could yous make us a loan for breakfast sir?"

The telegrapher reached into his pocket and handed Spats two silver dollars and ninety cents. "I'll stand the cost of the telegraph," he said. "Least I can do. Try the Miner's Café at the end of the street, on the corner of Sixth and Allen." The telegrapher turned and went back into the telegraph office closing the door behind him.

Spats held the money in his hand. Stuffing it in his pocket, he stood slowly and tried to help Mr. O'Brien to his feet.

Mr. O'Brien pulled his arm away from Spats' grip and angrily spew a stream of expletives Spats had never heard before. When he was done, Mr. O'Brien rose and started down the street towards the Miner's Café, stopping briefly to turn around to Spats. "Well, you coming? You seem to have all the money." Mr. O'Brien spun back around and again started off for the Miner's Café with Spats on his heels.

*****

The Hunter and Stryker were finishing saddling their horses and making ready to leave when Phineas Bellflower found them in their camp.

"Hunter, I don't know how to thank you. The assistance you have offered me has proven to be top notch and I really don't know how to repay you, or Mr. Stryker there." Phineas stood uneasily, shuffling his feet and not looking directly at either of the two men. "I have a confession. I was unable to sleep last night and I'm afraid I went into the bar at the Grand and treated myself quite heavily with the funds you afforded me."

The Hunter looked at Phineas and then over at Stryker. "Hell, Mr. Bellflower, we already figured you were gonna do that, and well deserved. No reason ta be sorrowful about it at all." The Hunter clapped Phineas on the shoulder. "Ya had a rough time of it for sure, you deserved a little fun I guess."

"Well, nonetheless Hunter, and I do thank you for your understanding, I took advantage of you and Mr. Stryker and I fully intend on repaying you just as soon as I can secure employment in Chicago." Phineas stuck out his hand and the two men shook hands. Then he pushed his hand out to Stryker. "Mr. Stryker, it has been a pleasure."

Stryker grasped Phineas' hand and shook it heartily. "Mr. Bellflower, you come back ta see us, meybe next time we won't, me and Mr. Hunter, won't drag ya across the desert so much." Stryker smiled at Phineas and released his hand.

"Would you gentlemen accompany me to the depot then?" asked Phineas.

Eastern Men

"It would be our honor sir." The Hunter put his hand on Phineas' shoulder. "Give us a minute to finish our packin."

Within a few minutes the Hunter and Stryker had finished their saddling, packed the mules and started from the small arroyo where they had been camping. With Phineas in tow, the three men started for the Wells Fargo depot.

*****

Whitey shook the sleep from his head and woke Lenny, lying beside him in the stable. "Hey, Lenny, wake up, I'm hungry as a bear comin from a winter's sleep."

Lenny rolled over in his blankets and looked at Whitey. "Did ya ever think that meybe, jest meybe, I ain't as hungry as you, Whitey?" Lenny sat up and raked his hair with his fingers.

"Did ya ever think that meybe, jest meybe, you got all the fuckin money, Lenny?" threw in Whitey. "We ain't et since day afore yestiddy and naturally I'm a bit hungry."

"Ah fuck, let me find a privy, then we'll go to that café we seen yestiddy, the 'Miner's' I think it was called." Lenny slowly rose from his blankets and went in search of a privy.

*****

Eastern Men

Michael McManus finished dressing and walked down the stairs of the Cosmopolitan Hotel. Walking to the desk, he found the desk clerk busy sorting mail for the individual boxes. Clearing his throat, McManus caught the clerk's attention. "Where is the best place for breakfast in town sir?"

"Why, here sir, unless you are looking for more base fare and then either Nellie Cashman's on Toughnut Street or the Miner's Café right down the street on the corner of Sixth and Allen Streets." The clerk said and resumed his sorting while glancing at McManus.

"Thank you sir," McManus said, turning to the door and leaving the hotel turning east toward Sixth Street and a bountiful breakfast.

*****

Spats and Mr. O'Brien were halfway to the café when Spats glanced across the street and spotted Michael McManus strolling towards the café as well.

Spats grabbed Mr. O'Brien by the arm. "Jamie, I know why they couldn't find Mr. McManus," he said.

"Yea, why would that be?" Mr. O'Brien replied.

Spats stopped and turned Mr. O'Brien toward the other side of the street and said, "Look!"

Eastern Men

Mr. O'Brien lifted his head and immediately spotted McManus walking the boardwalk. "Mickey, That's Mr. McManus! It's really Mr. McManus!" Mr. O'Brien exclaimed, loud enough for McManus to turn his head and spot the two men crossing the street to meet him.

McManus stopped and stared in wonderment at the two tattered and beat up men coming toward him. "If I didn't know better I would say you were Jamie O'Brien and Spats Melloy," said McManus.

"We are," replied Spats. "I guess there was no way we were gonna get a reply from you in Brooklyn, was there?" he asked.

"A reply to what," said McManus. What the hell are you two doing here and what in the world happened to you?"

At that moment Whitey and Lenny came out of the livery and started east to the café. Lenny caught sight of Spats and Mr. O'Brien.

Elbowing Whitey, Lenny had to cut loose. "Well looky, Whitey, there's them two eastern assholes agin…and they're talkin to another gent, what I strongly think is an asshole too."

"I'll be dipped in dog shit, Lenny, you're right. Whitey hitched up his trousers. "Wonder who the other asshole is?"

"Got no idea," said Lenny. "Truth is I ain't buyin em breakfast, that's for damn certain."

As they approached the café, Spats, Mr. O'Brien and McManus, the Hunter, Stryker and Phineas Bellflower came around the corner and right into the small group gathering outside the Miner's Café.

Phineas grabbed the Hunter's arm. "Hunter, there's the two I told you about," he said. Then he caught sight of Lenny and Whitey coming into view. "And Misters Wellford and Bristol as well." Stopping for a moment, he looked at McManus.

McManus, in shock and rage, turned to Spats and Mr. O'Brien. "Why the fuck is he still alive?" he roared. "And who the fuck are all these other people…Jesus Christ, I can't even send you to do a simple job like killing one fucking person."

"Don't know who the men are with Phineas, Mr. McManus, but the other two helped us out with the Apaches a while back," Mr. O'Brien answered.

"What Apaches?" asked McManus. "Never mind, I'll do it myself. McManus pulled a small .38 revolver from his pocket and started to point it at Phineas.

Before he could cock it, Stryker's Colt was pointed at McManus' face. "I like Mr. Bellflower, and I don't care what ya think he done, I like Mr. Bellflower and you ain't gonna shoot him, y'aint got the right."

"Young man, do you have any idea who I am?" McManus asked, looking at the big bore in the end of Stryker's Colt.

"No sir, ain't got no idea, and don't care. The truth stands, y'ain't gonna shoot him and that's that," replied Stryker. "It ain't right."

The Hunter moved forward and slowly took the pistol from McManus' grasp. "Looks ta me friend like you're outnumbered, unless these two here," he waved at Spats and Mr. O'Brien. "These two here want to get into the fray." The Hunter tossed the pistol to Phineas and turned to Spats and Mr. O'Brien. "I'm guessin yer Spats and Mr. O'Brien?"

"Yous would be right," replied Spats. "Who the hell are you two?"

"My manners," said the Hunter. "My name is Tag Richmond but most folks just call me 'Hunter', and the young man with the Colt in his hand, is Jeff Stryker. Now, do you two want to get into this?" *or not*

"Not us, we're going back to Brooklyn, which is slightly more hospitable than this God dammed territory," replied Mr. O'Brien. He turned to Phineas. "Phineas, sorry about everything. What you did wasn't so bad, in fact it was more the truth than anything." Mr. O'Brien turned to McManus. "I'll be troubling you for our wages, McManus, all of them we've got coming."

McManus sputtered but finally took his wallet from his pocket and withdrew a stack of bills, handing them to Mr. O'Brien.

When O'Brien had the money stashed in his pocket, he again looked at McManus. "We're going back to Brooklyn, McManus, but not to be with you. We are done with you and your lying, cheating and strong-arming. He turned to Phineas and motioned him over. Bending to his ear, he whispered something into Phineas' ear, turned on his heel and he and Spats walked into the café for a nice easy breakfast.

"Fuck them," McManus said and turned walking back to his hotel.

Whitey and Lenny, held transfixed with the threat of gunplay, quietly turned and tried to make an exit when Stryker stopped them

"Where ya goin boys?" asked Stryker. "You boys been a thorn in my saddle for awhile now, and ya durn near killed Mr. Bellflower here."

"O'Brien," said Phineas. "Phineas O'Brien is my name."

Eastern Men

The Hunter jerked his head around and looked at Phineas. "You mean to tell me…"

"The pronunciation of my name is actually Phin-ay-us and not Phin-e-us. I changed it when I went on to Chicago. I just thought Bellflower was a good handle." Phineas looked at the Hunter. "Jamie O'Brien is my brother. He's the bad one."

The Hunter and Stryker both were caught totally off guard by that confession. In a moment, Stryker looked back at Lenny and Whitey. "All right, Mr. O'Brien it is, but the name don't hardly matter, ya damn near killed him anyhow."

Whitey started to say something when the Hunter cut him off. "Don't bother Wellford, you ain't got no excuses. Truth is, we woulda hung ya in the desert if we'd a caught ya."

"What happened to all the money? We found the trunks and most of my things?" asked Phineas.

"Lost it in a flash flood a ways back," answered Lenny "Fuckin near lost us too."

"Yea," said Whitey. "We ain't had it too good neith…" Whitey stopped in mid sentence. "Ah shit," he said and elbowed Lenny.

Eastern Men

All the men turned and looked down the street where they spotted Deputy Sheriff Billy Breckenridge coming towards them.

"Mornin boys," said the deputy. "You do know that you can't be carrying firearms in town?" he asked.

"We know, we were just leavin, but these two," said the Hunter. "These two have something they want to tell you."

"No we ain't," said Whitey.

"I told you two before not to come back here," said Breckenridge. He looked at Stryker. "We ain't never met, but I know who he is," he said. "But who are you?"

"Jeff Stryker, deputy," answered Stryker. "I ride with Mr. Hunter."

"You the Stryker fella that took the Ghost down to Mexico?" asked Breckenridge?

"Yessir," replied Stryker.

Breckenridge nodded his head. Turning back to Whitey and Lenny he motioned for them to move. "Come on you two…it's to the jail for you."

Lenny looked over at Whitey. "I tolt ya, Whitey, I tolt ya Breckenridge would catch us…ya jest never listen ta me ya asshole."

Eastern Men

"Maybe in jail I can get some fuckin peace from you, Lenny, God knows I need it," responded Whitey.

"Let's go," said Breckenridge. And all three started down the street, Whitey and Lenny still arguing loudly.

The Hunter looked at Phineas. "Well, can't say this ain't been a fun four days Mr. Bell...uh, Mr. O'Brien." The Hunter chuckled. "Me and Jeff was just goin fishin anyhow."

Stryker walked to his packs and took his wallet pulling out some paper currency. Handing it to Phineas, he took off his hat. "You take this Mr. O'Brien. You pay me back when ya can. Yer gonna need it more than me, me, I got everything I need right here."

"Phineas accepted the money and shook Stryker's hand then turning, he shook the Hunter's hand and nodding, not wanting to prolong the departure, he turned and walked slowly to the stage depot.

The Hunter and Stryker watched him for a moment before mounting their horses and turning, rode west out of Tombstone towards the Circle-J and the Traces.

Eastern Men

Eastern Men

EPILOGUE

The San Pedro River was running high and the fishing had been excellent. The Hunter looked up from his seat by the fire and watched Stryker ride into camp. He had been in Tucson and the Bar-A to pick up necessities, mail and messages. Dismounting, Stryker squatted down and stretched out his leg muscles before standing and stretching long over his head. Not saying a word, he walked Waco to the line and unsaddled him and the mule pulling the packs and staking them by the Hunters.

When he was done with his grooming, feeding and watering he grabbed his saddle and gear and walked to the fire. "I wasn't sure I was gonna get back before dark. Glad I was wrong," he said. He found a suitable spot and tossed his gear down. Looking at the pot, his stomach started growling. "Anything left in the cook pot?"

"Help yourself," said the Hunter. "Any word from the Circle-J or Bar-A?"

"Billy Drewer says ta tell ya everything is good. I think he's takin to bein the ramrod there." Stryker thought for a moment then continued. "Mingo says that the new hand, Bountiful Jim, is all he said he was and more. Blacky is grumbling, but getting used to the fact Jim is there to

227

stay." He reached behind him and took a bundle from his saddlebags. "These I picked up in Tucson, don't know what they say, but they's for us I guess." Stryker tossed the packet to the Hunter and started spooning some food into a dish.

The Hunter took the packet and looked at the letters. There were four of them all from Phineas O'Brien and all from Chicago. "They're from Mr. Bell…" he caught himself. "Mr. O'Brien." He opened one of the letters addressed to him and read it quietly. It was a copy of the article Phineas had written about his travels in the Sonora Desert with the Hunter and Stryker. When he was done, he offered to read Stryker's to him and Stryker eagerly agreed.

The Hunter read Stryker's letters to him, the second one containing a sheaf of currency. When he was done he leaned back in the gathering darkness and looked at Stryker. "Not a bad fella, not bad at all," he finally said. "The whole time he was with us, I couldn't get him to understand about the Sonora is nuthin to fight. Accept her and you'll be fine. I guess it's hard for eastern men to get used to all the prickly biting things out here."

"I guess it's hard for some folks to get used to it, Mr. Hunter. It was hard for me, and Bobby, too, comin from were we come from and all. It was nice a Mr. O'Brien ta write stuff about us too…makes me feel a little strange." He shoveled a spoon full of food into his mouth. When he had chewed and swallowed, he looked up at the Hunter. "What did your other letter say Mr. Hunter?"

"It said he found his brother in Chicago, him and Spats, shot fulla holes so I guess he didn't give it up like he said." The Hunter adjusted his seat. "Shame about some people, it truly is."

"Yessir, it is, Syrus Common was a good man though," said Stryker, and he spooned another bite of food into his mouth.

"Heard he went back with Dick Gird, smart man. I don't think Gird will be accusing Syrus of anything ever again," said the Hunter. "What else ya bring Jeff?"

"Well sir, I picked up the new pair a chaps you had made, some ammunition, fish hooks…"

Slowly the night collapsed around the two friends enveloping them into it's folds.

Eastern Men

About the author:

Jim Christina is a, long time, living historian. He has written four other novels about the Hunter and Jeff Stryker and a two-act play, "An Evening With Tom Horn". He currently resides in Simi Valley, CA.

Eastern Men

Eastern Men

Eastern Men

Eastern Men

An excerpt from the new novel

Contraband Cowboys

by

Jim Christina

Eastern Men

Eastern Men

PROLOGUE

The hooded figure skirted around the outside of the small shack doubling as a barn. When he felt it was safe, he motioned for his comrades to join him in the darkness. As they waited, four of the hooded men wrapped rags around sticks, securing them with bailing wire and pouring kerosene on them.

When they were done, they sat back and waited for the signal. There was still a lamp lit in the small cabin and they were waiting for it to extinguish.

About ten minutes later, the lamp finally went out signaling to the masked marauders that the people in the house had retired for the night, yet, the group of men waited another half hour before moving.

When finally they did move, the ones holding the torches lit them and in a sudden rush, all of the men attacked the house firing wildly into the structure. As the firing increased, the four torches were thrown into the house and then they too drew their weapons and began firing into the small cabin.

As of yet, not a word had been spoken from either side, but now the sounds of screaming came from inside the cabin that was quickly turning into an inferno. And a lone figure jumped from the window, his shirt on fire and he was frantically trying to shake it off as he ran from the blaze. He managed to go twenty feet before several pistol balls found their target and he fell forward, grasping his chest as he fell.

In another second a tall man came out the door shouldering a shotgun and he too was cut down by the hooded men. They now knew there was only two more people in the cabin and they would have to come out quickly, or die in the flames.

Finally, a young woman, clasping a child in her arms, fought her way into the night and was grabbed by a tall burley man smelling of alcohol. She fought him and he slapped her hard across her face, almost knocking her out with the blow. Resigning herself, she allowed the child to be taken by the man and he handed the child to another man before turning back to the woman.

The man, apparently in charge, roughly grabbed the woman and dragged her to the barn. It was now, the woman knew, what was to be her fate. Resigned, she started making peace with her god, praying they wouldn't harm her infant son.

Three of the men walked to the barn and threw a loop over a bean by the small hayloft and let it drop, dangling by

Eastern Men

the woman's face. The big man again roughly grabbed the woman and pulled her arms behind her tying them tightly. One of the men rolled a rain barrel over and, turning it over, put it by the noose and the other two men lifted the woman onto the barrel slipping the noose over her neck. She had ceased to struggle and stood quietly on the barrel waiting for what she knew was to come.

"We warned you fuckin contraband darkies ta get outta the territory, and ya didn't heed us. We warned ya, and now we's gonna hang ya, but first, yer gonna watch this boy here," he snatched the wriggling baby from the man holding him. "Yer gonna watch your boy die, then you're gonna die hard." He held the boy over his head by the boy's ankles. The baby struggled and screamed in terror as the man began swinging the baby over his head, suddenly slamming the baby head first into the side of the small barn. The child was instantly quiet. The man dropped the infant to the ground and the woman couldn't stop the tears from streaming down her cheeks. She refused to give them what they wanted and that was showing her pain and fear.

"What's a matta bitch, not enough? Then go to fuckin hell." The man kicked the barrel out from under her, she dropped but not enough to break her neck, and she swung, slowly strangling at the end of the rope trying to

239

focus on her son laying in a heap at the edge of the building. As she began to die, she started dancing for air, searching for purchase but there was none to be had. In a few moments, she finally lost consciousness and all faded to black as her last thought was for redemption.

The men left her hanging there, at the barn, and they left the baby in the dirt, crumpled on the ground. One by one they turned and watched the rest of the cabin collapse into itself and slowly pulled their hoods from their heads.

"Another bunch that won't be around here no more," said one of the men. "Serves them right, they got no right ta be out here…fuckin contraband assholes."

The big man walked to his horse and withdrew a bottle from his saddlebags. Walking back to the others, he took and large drink and when he reached the others, he passed the bottle to them and allowed them a drink.

The smaller of the men picked up a stick and walked back to the woman that was now swinging slowly in the breeze, the rope quietly creaking with each sway of the body. Her tongue was blue and protruding from her mouth and her eyes bugged from their sockets. Her legs still jerked a small bit involuntarily as all life and energy left her body.

Eastern Men

The man took the stick and poked her, getting her to swing higher and faster. The man started giggling softly, eventually getting loud and almost sounding as if he were insane.

The big man took the last drink of the whiskey and threw the empty bottle in the smoldering ashes of what used to be a small cabin holding four lives. Turning, he motioned to all the others. "Let's go boys, we done our duty this night."

Together, to a man, they all filed back to their horses, mounted and headed back to the little town that had spewed them earlier in the evening.

Eastern Men

Eastern Men

ONE

Bountiful Jim rolled over on his bunk. Unable to sleep, he finally struggled out of bed, pulled on some trousers and boots and walked into the Arizona night. He loved this ranch. It was nothing like he expected when he signed on in Tombstone. All the buildings were neatly kept and freshly painted. The fences were in good repair and all the hands were friendly and helpful. It took him no time to fit in and Mingo Perez had, almost immediately, started using him on the bronc busting duties.

Jim worked hard as a hand and as a man. No one ever made a comment about his color and he never commented about theirs. All the hands on the 'A' were diverse. They had whites, blacks, Mexicans and a smattering of unknowns and all got along well. Each hand was respected for their abilities and their attitudes and that is precisely what made the work on the Bar-A not only acceptable, but highly sought after. And, it was well known that Mingo would ask you to join their crew, no one ever came in and asked for a job.

Walking out to the main corral, Jim pulled the braces from his trousers over his big shoulders and stood for a moment taking in the grace of the horses. Horses always amazed him, their power and ease of movement, their ability to carry a human for great distances, and, their willingness to do so.

But the letter from his brother bothered him. Bothered him deeply. It wasn't like his brother to complain and bother folks with his problems but this time he had reached out to Jim. Written a letter and expressed his fears and his concerns about some of the folks in the town he lived. Worried their actions and words might hold some truths and actions that he, Jim's brother, might not be able to handle.

Pushing away from the corral, Jim walked back to the privy to relieve himself then snuck back into the bunkhouse and laid back down on his bunk. When he was settled, a voice came out of the darkness.

"Yer sure restless Jim, somethin botherin ya?" the voice asked.

"Nah, not so much, Blacky," Jim answered. "Not so much bother as it is naggy." He sat back up in his bunk and looked over at Blacky. "I'm worried about some folks is all, Blacky. Jest a bit worried."

"You boys so rested you can sit up all night jawin?" Buck Simpson sat up rubbing his eyes. "Well, I ain't, so hows about you two either take it outside or shut the fuck up." He said.

Eastern Men

Jim looked over at Buck. "Sorry Buck, we'll shut up now and go ta sleep," he said. "Sides, I got me a heap a broncs in the mornin lookin ta bust my ass."

"That you have Jim, that you have. And if Mingo has anything ta say about it you'll be bustin them broncs til Christmas." Buck settled back into his bunk, shoving his arms behind his head. "Got a chill in the air. Meybe a bit early this year."

Blacky and Jim lay back on their bunks and closed their eyes. Presently Blacky sat back up and pulled on some trousers followed closely by Bountiful Jim. When they were both up and dressed they walked to Bucks bunk and without speaking, each man grabbed an end and upended Bucks bunk rolling him onto the floor.

"Come on you asshole, get up, let's go get Jasper and have some breakfast." Blacky stood back, knowing Buck could get prickly this early in the morning.

Buck shot up screaming. "You assholes!" he yelled. "Jest because you two cain't sleep, ya got no call ta be fuckin with the rest a us!" He reached down and righted his bunk, retrieved his pants from the floor and slipped them on, grabbing his boots, slipping them on as well. "Did I hear somethin about breakfast?" he asked.

Eastern Men

Farther into the morning as the hands were busy with their daytime duties, Charlie Jenkins paused for a moment, wiping his forehead and neck, with a kerchief, when he spotted a rider making his way into the valley from the butte.

Leaning on the shovel he was holding he watched as the rider got closer. Watched the gait he rode, the way he sat on the horse and the familiar picture of a man all too used to working in the saddle.

As the rider made his way into the ranch yard, Charlie leaned the shovel against the barn and walked to the front of the house. "Mornin friend. Can I help ya?" he asked.

The man was a black man, lean and sinewy. Charlie guessed medium height wearing the common range clothing of the cowboys in the Arizona Territory. The man pulled his bandana from his neck and wiped his face, re-tying the cloth around his neck

"Y'all got a hand here name a Bountiful Jim?" he finally asked.

Charlie looked at the man for a moment. "Yea," he answered. "We got a Bountiful Jim here, what business you got with him?"

The rider eyed Charlie all the while looking around the ranch. "He's my brother is all," he said. "A man can visit his brother I guess."

Eastern Men

Charlie looked again at the rider and now realized the resemblance to Jim. Relaxing, Charlie moved closer to the rider. "Step down sir. My name is Charlie Jenkins and I'm the caretaker here on the Bar-A." Charlie moved to the horse and grabbed the lead hanging from the halter. "Step down friend, rest a while."

The rider folded his reins over the saddle horn and dismounted. Extending his hand he said, "Lewis Bishop," he said. "Glad ta meet ya Mr. Jenkins."

"Charlie," said Charlie. "Just Charlie." He paused a minute before resuming. "So, Bishop is Jim's last name. We all been wonderin around here since he got here. Now we know."

"That ain't exactly right," said Lewis. "We had different pa's. His was a Mr. Lent. He died afore I was born, then ma married my pa."

"Ah, so Jim's name is Lent then?" asked Charlie.

"Yessir, it sure is," replied Lewis. "Now, think I could see my brother?

Charlie walked Lewis' horse to the hitch and tied him off. Turning to Lewis, he took his arm and both men started walking towards the big round pen used for bronc breaking.

When they arrived, they both leaned on one of the rails and watched as Jim took the bronc, he was then breaking, for a few spins around the pen. With one mighty heave, the horse managed to buck violently and Jim lost his seat, launching into the air and coming down on his butt in a cloud of dust, he had to crab wiggle out of the way while the horse refused to stop the rampage.

Climbing over the rails, Jim pulled his hat from his head and dusted himself off, then he noticed Charlie and…could it be, really? His brother Lewis standing with Charlie grinning at him.

"Lent huh?" asked Charlie. "Your secret is out Jim."

"Ain't no sense tryin ta keep anything from you assholes," Jim grinned and looked at Lewis. "And you, you horse turd, what are ya doin here?"

Lewis walked to Jim and the two men hugged. Stepping back and looking at him, Lewis shook his head. "You look good brother, you really do."

"You too, but you ain't here ta make me feel good, I thought we decided you was gonna stay put in Yavapai County with yer pa and Felice." Jim leaned on a rail and pulled a long sliver, sticking it in his mouth.

Lewis started moving some dirt with his foot and took a long time before he finally looked at Jim. "We did," he said. "We did say that, but things kinda changed Jim." Lewis turned away and wiped a tear starting at the corner of his eye. Turning back to Jim, he put his hand on his brother's shoulder. "They kilt em Jim, kilt em all while I was gatherin the cattle for brandin."

The shock of Lewis' words slammed into Jim as the reality of what his brother had just said settled over him. "Kilt who Lewis, who kilt who?"

Lewis was now wracked with sobs and Jim waited a bit before he put his arms around his brother and pulled him in close to him. All their lives they had been close. Close like full brothers, in fact, Jim had never thought of Lewis as anything other than his brother, and Felice had never been anything but his sister. The enormity of what Lewis had just told him caused his breath to catch in his throat and a small moan to escape from him as he held his brother while he sobbed.

Charlie yelled at his daughter, Olympia, as she walked from the house to the barn. "Olympia, Olympia, come here!"

Olympia walked to her father and stopped putting her hand on her hips exactly like her mother did. "Pa, ma says I have ta get the eggs from the coop before she whollops me a good one."

"Right now, your gonna get on a horse and go get Mingo. I'll take care a your ma," said Charlie. "Hurry now."

Eastern Men

Olympia looked at Jim and the other man embracing with the one man sobbing and instinctively she knew this was no time to argue. Taking off at a run, she went into the barn and five minutes later came out leading a small pinto horse. Jumping up on his back, Olympia galloped out of the gate and turned west to get Mingo.

Charlie poured more coffee into their cups and sat back in his chair. The story he had just heard chilled him to the bone and he knew, beyond everything else, Jim was going with Lewis to right this horrible wrong. In that way, Jim was a lot like the Hunter and Stryker. Had a sense of right and wrong and a strong desire to make things right.

The two brothers were sitting talking about their sister, Lewis' father and their nephew when Mingo opened the door and came into the kitchen.

"Now, what's all this about? God dammit, I got two hunnert horses on the range and damn few hands ta keep em quiet...Jim why ain't ya bustin them broncs like we talked about?" Mingo stopped and looked at Lewis. "Who are you?" he asked and sat heavily in a chair.

When Lewis was finished with his story, Mingo leaned back in his chair. Picking up his cup he drained his coffee putting the cup back on the table. "Lewis, I know what it's like ta loose folks. The Barretts here was like kin ta me, like Jim is ta you." Mingo thought a second then resumed. "A course Jim is goin back with ya, ain't no other way. If I can get a hold of Mr. Hunter; I'll let him know too. But," he paused a moment. "Buck is goin with ya," Buck paused. "Ain't no arguing…he's good with a gun and levelheaded. Buck is goin that's final."

Jim looked at Mingo. "You know I'll be back right?"

"I know you'll be back Jim. Never thought anythin else," answered Mingo.

Two hours later, three men rode out of the Bar-A. Buck Simpson, Bountiful Jim Lent and Lewis Bishop. All men with a purpose, all men with their minds set to one conclusion. Make right the terrible wrong visited on the family of Bountiful Jim and Lewis Bishop.

Eastern Men

Made in the USA
Charleston, SC
20 November 2010